The Servant of the Manthycore

Michael Ehart

Advance Praise for *The Servant of the Manthycore*!

"Reminiscent of the classic sword and sorcery tales by **Robert E. Howard** and **Michael Moorcock**, Ehart's yarn of servitude and choice is finely crafted. A vivid setting, a strong, intelligent heroine, a moody atmosphere... The ending is wickedly fun."

Paul Abbamondi, Tangent Online

"Behold a warrior woman as ruthless, bloody, and honorable as the ancient world in which she walks, spanning more than forty lifetimes, while Ur and Babylon seethe with a thousand gods.... What we have here is no less than a bright new epic, written with the bold spirit of the 21st century, yet spanning back into the mists of time. From Michael Ehart's fierce imagination comes an unforgettable gritty heroine, both human and goddess, and yet something much more.... Gilgamesh, Elric, and Conan have finally met their female match!"

Vera Nazarian, author of *Dreams of the Compass Rose* and *Lords of Rainbow*

"Michael Ehart's "Servant" stories are thrilling, involving, surprising, and complex. The smell, touch, and taste of Bronze Age life come through sharply, clearly, with the tang of authenticity and the gritty detail of thorough research not just thought through but ***felt*** through. His sword-wielding heroine scythes down opponents like they were bad ideas, moving from episode to episode as gracefully and inevitably as death itself.
Also, these stories are just plain ***fun*** to read."

Nisi Shawl, co-author of *Writing the Other*

"Fast-paced, richly detailed, good, clean bloodthirsty fun."

Elizabeth Ann Scarborough

“Michael Ehart transports the readers of The Servant of the Manthycore back to a fantasy Bronze Age Mesopotamia. In this world, the Manthycore is a sorcerous Beast who feeds on human flesh. For centuries, the servant has served the Manthycore "in bitter unwillingness," until she has forgotten her own name and become an immortal legend in her own right: the Betrayer. Long ago, she fought to free her captive lover, but now, after so many centuries, she has come to seek death as the only way to be free of her curse. If she can only find a warrior skilled enough to defeat her - and the Manthycore. ...even the gods hate and fear the Manthycore.”

Lois Tilton, Author of *Written in Venom*

“Instead of the Tolkien emulation, so beloved even now by many authors, Ehart instead takes a far calmer, historical approach to his world. There are no guilds here, no huge kingdoms, just people trying to make their way and leave their mark. It's a stylistic move that reminded me a lot of David Gemmell's work; there's the same gritty, personal feel to the story that Gemmell brings to his work.”

Alasdair Stuart, Tangent Online

The Servant of the Manthycore

Michael Ehart

Double-Edged Publishing

Cordova, Tennessee

www.doubleedgedpublishing.com

ISBN 13: 978-0-9793079-5-9
ISBN 10: 0-9793079-5-3

Library of Congress Control Number: 2007939459

Double-Edged Publishing, Inc.
9618 Misty Brook Cove
Cordova, Tennessee 38016

For the word of God is living and active. Sharper than any double-edged sword, it penetrates even to dividing soul and spirit, joints and marrow; it judges the thoughts and attitudes of the heart.

Hebrews 4:12 New International Version (NIV)

www.doubleedgedpublishing.com

Printed in the United States of America
First Printing

-= For Shaharazahd =-

Foreword

In the fine tradition of Mary Renault, Henry Treece, Thomas Burnett Swann or Rex Warner, Michael Ehart has given us an outstanding story of the ancient world. This is a narrative concerning the fantastic unlike most books published today as fantasy fiction. It resonates with the authenticity of genuine myth, bringing a deep, true sense of the past; a conviction which does not borrow from genre but mines our profoundest dreams and memories; the kind which give birth to myths. As Ehart's protagonist, the beautifully realized warrior woman sometimes known as Ninshi, tells us "Songs all end up right. Life does not." Yet, as she demonstrates, it is part of the human condition that we are forever striving to make things end up like the songs.

This novel demonstrates the difference between a good folk tale, a genre story, and an enduring myth. The genre story usually dodges the facts of genuine tragedy while the myth, or the story which retains the quality of myth, does not.

Michael Ehart's story of dark bloodshed, torment and betrayal invokes the earliest civilizations of Mesopotamia, of Ur and Babylon, set against landscapes we all now know so well from our nightly news bulletins. These are the places where our oldest mythologies began and where our youngest ones are now being created. He provides us with telling images as well as some tremendous descriptions, none more so than the terrifying monster of the title.

This is a grim and gripping tale appealing to all of us who grew up fascinated by our Indo-European heritage, by Fraser's *Golden Bough* or Graves's *White Goddess*, by Zoroaster and the Epic of Gilgamesh or tales of the Minotaur, even Beowulf and The Green Knight.

This book is a thoroughly engaging page-turner. It's a very long time since I read a fantastic tale as good as this. Michael Ehart is an impressive talent.

-- ***Michael Moorcock***

The Servant of the Manthycore

Michael Ehart

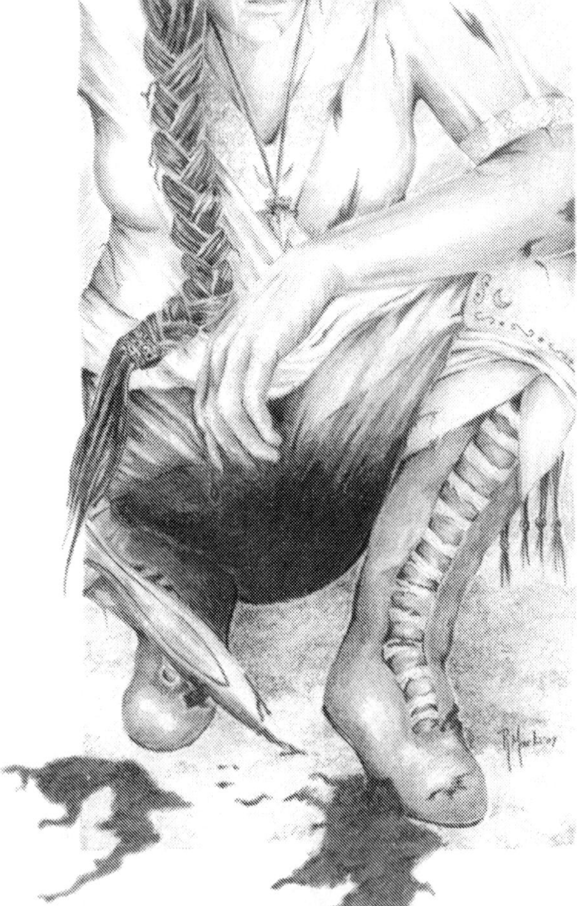

Through My Tears

Voice of the Spoiler

I sat on the bare rock, weeping as the blood dripped from my lowered hand to form small, black balls in the dust. Through my tears I saw the scuffed grey toe of my boot, spattered with gore. The oilwood hilt of my sword, dropped in a puddle of its own making. Red dust. And the outstretched hand of Olveg, which still twitched lightly in death. A pariah dog barked somewhere. A hawk, or perhaps a sunbird, cried behind me over the plain of Aturia.

Olveg was a follower of the Ugarit Masked God, whose followers seem to expect treachery, and so should have been more suspicious. In fact, it was Olveg who died last, the only one who even suspected the trap that left only me alive. I raised my head.

One of Olveg's heavy boots was stubbed against Tovar's head. The rest of Tovar was several feet away, his thickly-muscled frame slumped against the rocky dirt wall of the wadi. I had hoped for more from him, too, a scarred veteran of a dozen wars between the Cities of the Plain. He was quick and tough, with an old soldier's cynical eye.

Uhlma of Nineveh and his servant, whose name I already could not remember, lay in twin heaps where they fell. They were worthless. Their deaths didn't cause enough of a delay or outcry to warn the others.

I sighed and wiped my eyes with my sleeve. My arm was no longer bleeding. Already the wound was closing; soon it would be just another scar. Stiff for a while, but not enough to keep me from the unpleasant task before me. I knelt beside Olveg and unfastened his blood-soaked tunic. Soon all four were naked, laid out side-by-side in a neat line, Tovar's severed head resting on his chest.

I stepped back and pulled the talisman by its chain from under my tunic where it seared against my bare flesh. It was red, its broken-tooth shape stained by blood. My blood.

I held it up against the afternoon sun and cleared my thoughts. Come, I called silently. *Come*.

The young couple was playing lover's hide-and-seek under the cherry trees when they heard the cries. She was first to react. She put her hands to his lips to stifle his giggle, and ran to where the two of them had left their bows. There was peace in the land this spring, but it wasn't always so, so neither was ever very far from weapons.

He was quick and beat her to the stack of gear piled under a tree. He handed her a bow, then strung his. With silent signals they quickly agreed on a plan, and separately made their way through the orchard to the road.

Just a few minutes before the road had been empty. Now it was filled by struggling bodies, waving swords and other weapons. Two men were already down and two more quickly joined them, leaving a robed man waving a spear at three men armed with swords. The situation required little experience or wisdom to understand. It was an ambush by bandits, and going quite well for them, too.

There was no real reason why the boy did what he did next; he simply did it. The first arrow was no more than halfway to its target before the second was on its way.

The hum of a bowstring off to his left let him know she had followed his lead. Two of the bandits fell and the third ran off, the ambushers ambushed.

By the time they made to the robed man's side he had already collapsed. The girl made him a pillow of a discarded pack and the boy tried to get him to take a little water. It was clear to all three that he was dying.

"You've seen this before," the man said.

The boy nodded. Young as he was, he had already marched from Ugarit in punitive campaigns against the western savages. He had seen many men wounded far less seriously than this who didn't live, and he had no illusions of this one's chances.

"Boy, there is something you can do for me and for yourself." The man clawed at the chain around his neck, and pulled out a talisman shaped like a tooth. The effort made him cough and he had difficulty stopping. His voice was weaker when he regained it. "Have you heard of the Manthycore?"

Nippur was a trade center, the place where the East-West road met the Great River Euphrates. Things were very busy with the spring trade fair. Thousands, perhaps tens of thousands, of merchants, buyers and their guards, ox-drivers, servants and whores converged between the gates and the canal.

I was here before, but long enough ago that I was likely forgotf, even by those who still lived. It was dirty even as cities go, wet, muddy and with an entire population that seemed only to be passing through. Even by spending more than I safely should, I was only able to get half a room in a second-rate caravansary.

Still, I have done some of my best work in second-rate places and this one was no exception. The public room was packed with caravan guards, paid off now and wallowing in the luxury of temporary wealth. By the time a week had passed, some would be dead, many more in jail and a happy few at work on their way to the next city. The rest would most likely turn to banditry, thus justifying the employment of their luckier brothers.

I chose my table with care. From long experience with places like this I knew the greatest danger sits at the quietest table.

In this case the quietest table was in the far corner, against the hearth of an empty fireplace. It was occupied by four men and there was a clear space around them, a space carefully maintained by cautious neighbors. A good sign.

Another good sign was how carefully I was watched as I made my way across the crowded room to them. Along the way I scooped up a stool, perhaps left on its side by some altercation, and setting it upright at the table, sat down uninvited.

The largest man, armed but harnessed as a servant, growled and stood up. I ignored him. The man beside him restrained him with a touch and he sat back down. Other than that, there was no visible reaction to my invasion.

No visible one but it was a safe bet that under the table weapons were drawn or otherwise made ready. This was a tough, experienced looking crew and no tipstaff or thief-catcher was going to take them unaware.

"I have work," I announced. With my left hand I threw a small purse onto the table. My right never left the oilwood hilt of my sword. "High pay, great danger, long journey, bad company."

They laughed. The oldest, a heavily scarred man of forty or so, leaned forward.

"High pay?" he asked, and smiled.

"But we have the talisman!" he cried, in the hundredth installment of the argument which carried them through forty days of travel, to the heart of the Eastern Waste. "It is only a matter of will!"

She smiled as she shook her head. "I still say the best course is to sneak in and sneak out and not take any chance of being caught."

He flushed, and replied hotly. "And no chance of catching any glory, either!" And then smiled, embarrassed.

She smiled back. Though they had argued this many times neither had ever grown angry. This was the sort of great adventure that tales were told of and both were young enough to fully savor the romance of it all.

She reached over her horse to touch his hand where it rested on the pommel of his saddle. "Either way, we will be richer than any king," she smiled. "And richer even still, together."

With the belongings of the bandits, they had purchased horses at the next village. Never really admitting that such was the plan, their path had gradually found its way to the east, where the fabled Manthycore guarded a great sorcerer's treasure.

"All we must do is face it down. It is after all only a beast. And with the talisman we can commune with it direct." He leaned over and kissed her. "Just like that, only less sweet."

She laughed and kissed him back, hard.

"A matter of will!" she teased.

I sat at the edge of the fire-glow, working a stone against the bronze of my sword. The point required special attention, as always, and the light was not so good here. I could have moved closer to the fire but that would have meant joining my companions.

I ignored the crunch of Olveg's heavy boots in the gravel. We were camped in a long dry streambed. Its small banks provided some relief from the wind.

Olveg sat next to me. He had tried to insinuate himself into my good graces ever since we left the city. It was fruitless. I have no graces, good or otherwise.

He was a very suspicious man, a product of the cult of the Masked God. The God's followers believe that everyone is out to get them, including their God. The Masked God regularly betrays his own followers to the other gods for whatever temporary advantage it gains Him.

"That is a beautiful sword!" he exclaimed, and sat on the bank next to me. He had learned that if he waited for an invitation that is all he would do. Wait, that is.

"I am certain that I have never seen one of such curious design. Does not that heavy point make it difficult to wield?"

I continued to work the blade with the stone. Over by the fire, Uhlma was singing an old plains caravan song about a beast, a hero, his companions and a quest. I have heard this song many times over the years. It is a good song, but the story is all wrong.

I looked up at Olveg. Better to talk to him than to listen to that song. "Yes, it does make it difficult at first." I put down the stone, wiped the blade and slid it into the oiled wolf-skin scabbard.

"But with practice the advantages soon outweigh the awkwardness." I stood up and brushed myself off.

"Like all such things, it is a matter of will."

The boy lifted the talisman over his head, just as he had been taught by the man on the road. It was hard, this clearing of thoughts. His excitement kept getting in the way.

The girl stood behind him, almost dancing with anticipation. Every few minutes she reached out to him, and was barely able to keep herself from tapping him on the shoulder.

Finally, it was too much. "Is it working?" she asked in a loud whisper.

His shoulders dropped in exasperation. He turned around to glare at her, but her face was so alight with excitement that his heart melted and he found himself smiling instead.

"It will if you'll stop interrupting me!" he laughed. He reached out and patted her cheek. "Go sit over there on that rock, and I'll try again."

She laughed back at him and stepped away from the cave entrance where he stood.

He turned around and faced the dark cave-mouth. Holding the talisman high, he once more tried to clear his thoughts. *Come*, he called silently. *Come*.

At the first rustling in my mind, I stepped back from the bodies and lowered the talisman. I wanted as little direct contact as possible. Even so, that slightest of brushings was hideously painful, like having daggers thrust into my ears, eyes and heart all at the same time.

By the time I could see again it had already begun to feed. As always it started with the soft parts. The belly and the face are its favorites and because it feeds so seldom it showed little restraint. This time it chose to wear the head of a lion, which seemed to be well suited for the task.

It felt the force of my gaze, but did not react right away, engrossed in some particularly savory morsel from the belly of one of the corpses. I was careful not to take note of which one. It is a matter of pride that I not look away but I long ago learned to look without seeing.

Eventually it looked up, blood dripping from its muzzle. "This one is damaged."

In order to speak it transformed the lion's mouth to something more human. The gore remained, smearing its half-lion visage.

"Yes, he was suspicious and a little quicker than I expected. The others were no problem."

"You will do better, next time." It lowered its head, features already flowing back to fangs and jowls.

"Next time?" Although expected, it still hurt to know my hopes were vain. "I thought perhaps, finally...."

It formed an extra mouth on the top of its head, so as to talk without interrupting its ghastly feast. "No, I think not. Perhaps next time."

Next time. I felt like weeping again, but willed not to show it my weakness. At the same time the old, bitter hope rose, even though I knew that it was based on a lie. Still....

"Will you at least let me see?" I asked, not wanting to beg, but only just keeping myself from doing so.

It grunted what I first took to be a refusal, but even as my heart sank there was a glimmering at the edge of the wadi.

It was as though a window opened in the bank onto a small room. It was furnished with large pillows and rich hangings, but I had no attention for those.

My gaze, my whole world, was filled with the youth who lounged there. He was tall, with black, curly hair, a wide mouth given much to laughter. He was as beautiful as I remembered, dressed in the same clothing he has worn these past three hundred years, unchanged from that day at the mouth of the cave of the Manthycore.

"This is true?" I asked. "Not just a sending, but him truly as he is?" The beast didn't answer. It never does, though I ask each time.

I drank the sight of him in, but soon, too soon, the glimmering faded and the window closed.

I stood for a while, staring at where he was. Eventually I was able to move again, and started to gather my gear. I had already gone through the leavings of the others, tucking what looked useful or valuable into my pack. I ignored the sounds the beast made behind me as it dined.

I started back down the wadi, to where the horses were tethered. One of them was better than mine, and so I decided to keep it when I sell the rest.

Next time. Next time I will select an even tougher band. One not so easily taken from behind. Better swordsmen, who are not so easily slain by a woman, even a woman with three hundred years experience. Instead of being killed, they will kill me, and then kill the Manthycore. And my love will be free.

Next time.

It is a matter of will.

The Darkness Solidified

The Servant of the Manthycore

For at least a quarter day, I knew that there was death ahead.

It was a feeling at first, even before I saw the sunbirds circling the spot of green on the plain below. Down from the hills, and closer, I could smell it on the occasional quartering wind.

The oasis was known to me. It was seldom-used, a stop on an odd leg of the caravan route. In dry years the spring was brackish and foul, and the discomfort of the route and the lack of secondary trade opportunities generally outweighed the day or two gained by the slightly shorter distance traveled between Carcamesh and Mari. Most traffic was by the Euphrates road instead.

The feeling grew stronger as I approached. Around my neck, the broken-tooth talisman throbbed. It knew death. So did I.

I dismounted and made the last thousand steps afoot. Closer, the mare shied. I stopped to tie her lead rope to a large rock. I pulled my sword from the wolf-skin scabbard hanging from the saddle. Holding it with the heavy point down, I slowly made my way to the first line of trees where the red dust gave way to the grey-green saw grass of the oasis floor.

The wind soughed through the sparse trees. In the clearing near the spring stood a black tent, half erected. A loose corner flapped against a tent-pole. A sunbird croaked above. Another hopped away as I approached, bloated full and unable to fly. The camel it had been feeding on lay outside of the square of ancient broken brick that surrounded the tent. Inside the tumbled wall were smaller lumps with torn scraps of silk flapping weakly from them.

The wind shifted fully and the stench hit me. I swallowed, tried to spit. For a moment, I was able to distract myself with the dapple of late-afternoon sun reflecting from the bronze of my sword. Then I surrendered to the heave of my stomach and bent to cover the nearby stones with my midday meal.

Finally I was able to straighten. I wiped my mouth on the sleeve of my tunic, started toward the spring to rinse my mouth, thought better of it. I spat several times, thinking ruefully of the water skin tied to my saddle a hundred paces behind me.

I circled around the tent, stepping over the crumbling old brick of the ruined wall behind. Packs and bales lay in a neat, undisturbed heap in an angle of better-preserved wall. Once there was a caravansary here, never prosperous and generations gone. I had stayed here twice, perhaps eighty years apart.

I sat down on a bale of silks, sword across my knees, and pondered. I could tell nothing from the bodies. The sunbirds had taken their fill.

Bandits had not taken this caravan. Their goods were intact, not looted. Unless all the bandits had died in the raid as well. Unlikely.

From the smell and the looks of the corpses, whatever had happened was two or three days gone. If it were poisoned or tainted water, there would be dead sunbirds as well. I saw none. Still, I would not drink or eat here.

What did that leave? Sudden insanity, wild beasts, sorcery.

I have traveled this land for lives of men. While I have heard many songs at fireside, and tales told in wine shops of packs of savage beasts who hunger after man-flesh, I really only know of one beast who truly feasts in that fashion. And it never hunts, preferring its meat to be brought to it. One man, perhaps, or a camel or horse brought down by a lion I could believe. Not an entire caravan.

I have seen, in the land of the Khettites, in the city near where the two seas join, packs of men who in a state of religious ecstasy attack themselves and each other, tearing flesh, self-castrating, bleeding, singing, laughing, and dying in homage to their obscure god on his feast day. But we were far from there and theirs is a poverty cult, not likely to be favored by merchants.

I didn't like what that left. The talisman that hung from my neck told me little. It throbbed, yes, but from the nearness of death or from the residue of sorcery, I couldn't tell. Likely both.

I checked the sun. It was only a hand's-breadth now from the horizon. I wouldn't camp here. Too likely to draw larger carrion eaters, though that it hadn't already was another curiosity. And whatever or whoever had killed a dozen armed men and their beasts might still be around.

I picked up an armload of firewood on my way back to where my mare waited, shifting uncomfortably against the restraint of the lead rope. I tied the wood into a bundle and lashed it to her back. I led her around the oasis until the lengthening shadows made the uneven ground uncertain. I hobbled her, rubbed her down, fed her a few hands full of grain, and splashed water from one of the water skins into a shallow hollow in a rock for her to drink.

By full dark I had a small fire going. I ate nothing myself. The memory of the stench was too near. There was another thing too. Instead of fading as we moved farther away from the carnage behind us, the throbbing of the talisman had grown stronger, more insistent. Usually it only does that when it is in the presence of the Manthycore, whom I serve with bitter unwillingness, but serve nonetheless. Death and sorcery make it live and the Manthycore is both.

I sat facing the fire, my back to a large stone. My sword was again on my lap. The night filled with the small sounds of the dry plains between the rivers. Rustlings, night-bird cries, the chirp of a mouse. Overhead, thin clouds moved quickly over a waning half-moon and covered and revealed the tired stars.

I felt the presence a moment before I heard the change in the night noises. All of the regular activity of the night ceased. A half-beat later, I heard the flap of wings coming from the direction of the oasis. I expected the mare to bolt but she didn't react at all. For a moment the moon was hidden by a dark form that drifted toward me, covering in turn the stars in a great, irregular patch. The edges rippled where they were outlined against the scattered stars and the flapping sound grew louder and slower.

And then stopped, perhaps fifty paces away. It had landed.

Then the mare reacted. She tried to bolt, caught hobbled, and fell. I expected her to scream, as panicked horses will, but she was silent except for her panting and the thump and scrabble of rocks and soil knocked loose by her struggle to rise.

I kept my eyes ahead.

I rose to my feet, keeping my eyes on the thickening darkness ahead. I balanced my weight evenly on both feet, rising slightly on my toes, knees bent. I took three or four quick breaths to charge my lungs, then slowed my breathing. I held my sword at an angle across my body, point out and slightly down.

And waited.

The small breeze shifted. With the shift came the stench of death, of a thousand deaths—horrible deaths, the smell of pain and blood, rotting flesh, festering wounds, and ruptured bowels.

I grimaced. "I think you know me," I called. "And if you do, you must know that smell will not drive me in fear or turn my guts to water. I know that smell. I do not fear it, but it does make me foul-tempered."

There was a chuckle from the darkness ahead—low, feminine, throaty. "That would not be entirely desirable, I think," the voice said. "I have stopped it. The wind will carry it away. I didn't think it would frighten you, but you know how it is..."

I waited. Though I had spoken, nothing had moved except my mouth. I was still at ready. The reek blew to tatters in the breeze, faded, and was gone.

"Well," the voice said. "Will you invite me to your camp?"

"I will not," I replied. "I'll not have you as my guest. But you may approach, if you must."

There was a sigh, and then a wry chuckle, perhaps a little forced. The darkness solidified even further and shrank until it coalesced into the form of a woman, dressed in the fashion of a southern people long vanished, dark strips of camel's wool wound about her slender frame. Heavy as her garments were, her arms, bosom, and face were bare. On one arm was a coil of black—sometimes still and made of ebony, the next moment a small black snake. On her other arm was a wide black leather band. On it perched a small, black vulture.

She was pale, with black hair and eyes. Her skin was smooth and flawless.

Once, very long ago, my skin had that milk-like texture too. The tracks of centuries and death were written on my face now, and though I had not aged a day in nearly 40 lifetimes of man, no one would ever again think me young.

Or find me beautiful, as she was.

"You are the servant of the Manthycore," she said. "I have come a great distance and wrought much to speak with you."

"Your handiwork?" I asked, nodding in the direction of the oasis without taking my eyes from her.

She laughed again, this time with real delight. "I thought it might get your attention. And this far from my home, it doesn't hurt to re-establish my... authority."

Behind me, my horse had ceased her kicking and was still. Her breathing was heavy, panting. I wondered if her heart would burst. I did not wish to be afoot here, so far from any likely replacement.

"I am Ananth," she announced. She paused, as if she expected me to be awestruck by her revelation. She could wait all she liked. I am sometimes struck, but seldom by awe.

After a few moments she frowned. "Perhaps you don't know of me. I have been long away from this land."

"I know you." She truly had been long from this land. Her people had been driven out by one of the Sargons, long before my birth. There were still tales that had frightened me as a little girl, and songs. And occasionally travelers might come across her image—

serpent on one arm, vulture on the other—scratched into a stone where once a temple stood.

"Then you know what I can do. I require a service of you."

"I am in service to another, bitter though it is, and sadly must refuse."

"What if I could free you of that service?"

What was that feeling that jumped in my breast? How long had it been since someone had offered me hope? For over 400 years, I had served the Manthycore, the great sorcerous beast, devourer of man-flesh. As a foolish child I had come with my lover, armed with the talisman that rested on my chest, on a great quest for a treasure held by a foul beast. Since then he had held me in servitude, and held the boy I love unchanged, to compel me. To preserve my lover I lure warriors and ruffians to secluded places and kill them so the Manthycore might feed on fresh meat. He does not specify that I bring him those who can fight; I do.

For the first few years it was because having had my innocence stolen, I could not bring myself to steal the life of any who still had that fragile commodity. Then, when I came to believe that the beast would never honor our pact and someday release my love from his captivity, I began seeking out those who through strength of arm might instead slay him.

I became the measure. Sorcery could not touch me. The talisman that kept me young protected me, healed my wounds, and summoned the Manthycore to his dreadful feasts. Many lifetimes of men spent fighting made me difficult to slay. And few men ever believed that a mere woman, no matter how scarred, could ever out-fight them.

Someday, I thought, I would find a man or group of men who could slay me. If they could kill me, then perhaps they could kill the Manthycore. My love and I would both be free then. But generations had fallen beneath my sword, and the long, weary years had passed.

But now, hope! Long practice at revealing nothing made my face still, but my thoughts raced.

"What if you could? And what do you know of my service?"

"I know what the songs tell, that you are a slayer of men in service of an ancient beast who has consumed men since before the days of Eniku and the great deluge. I know that there was a young man, once, and may still be. I know that none in these decadent days of city-dwellers and silk-draped men can stand in combat against you. Some say you are a goddess, as am I, one of the ten thousand gods of these lands."

I shook my head. "I am no goddess, nor would I desire to be one."

"There are those who worship you, you know. Those who say that you are me, returned to this land. You could have that, if you desired. You could be at my right hand."

"And for this you desire for me to kill for you."

She smiled again. "It is what you do, after all. And this is such a small thing. There is a man, an old man, from Chaldea. He travels with his family and retainers. Some call him The Well Digger."

"I know him."

"You traveled with him for a time, did you not?"

"For a time."

For several weeks I had traveled with this old man she spoke of. He was a holy man, of sorts, who spoke of a single god, a creator god, wise, powerful and above the pettiness and small behaviors of mortals, yet concerned with their lives, their treatment of each other and their faithfulness in all things. I could not quite believe in this god of his, but when I left him I no longer believed in the gods I had before. They had not answered my only prayer. The Well Digger had explained that his god would not answer me either—not from indifference, but because he reserved vengeance for himself.

"Why him?" I asked.

She smiled. "He talks too much. Perhaps someday his talk will inspire others. The gods are only as strong as we are believed to be."

"And why me?"

"You are a great slayer of men. I would have you serve me. I am not a goddess of combat, though I love it. Why should others gain from deaths that you create?"

"And so to serve you...?"

"Slay this Well Digger, then together we shall slay the Manthycore."

"No."

"No?" She seemed amazed.

"No."

"How can one who has lived so long be such a fool! I offer you freedom and a place by my side!"

"You offer what I offer. Death. If you could kill this man, he would be dead. But he is protected somehow. Even I could sense that. You hope to destroy a rival. Either of us dead would do that."

"A rival? I am a goddess!"

"That men think you one does not make it so. Some men think me one, as you said. I am no more goddess than you. You are a sorceress or priestess grown old on the blood of others, that's all. Perhaps to some I am displacing you."

She laughed, perhaps the first genuine thing she had done. "Vain fool. If not in life, then serve me in death!"

The reek slammed into me like a runaway camel. At the same time, there was a shuffling and steps in the dark. I had time for a breath, and then they were upon me.

I had never seen dead men walk, but from the tales I expected stumbling and clumsiness. Not so. They were fast—fast, and deadly sure with their spears and blades. In life they had been caravan guards and merchants. In death they were demon warriors; torn, hideous and bloated, but quick and deadly.

I slashed left at the first spear thrust. My sword jolted against the haft, severing it just behind the head. Whirling, I evaded another from my right, and parried a sword slash at my head. I returned a disemboweling stroke.

The swordsman did not fall.

Dead already, he did not fall.

And then I was submerged in a cataract of cutting, dodging, slashing, and parrying.

There were more than ten of them, however many had been in the caravan. They were too many, even for me. But the rock at my back kept them from behind me, and their very speed and ferocity kept them from facing me any more than three or four at a time.

And I have been doing this for a very long while.

For a time, I was lost in the glee and certainty that I was wrong. That she could slay me. That the

Manthycore would finally be defeated and my lover freed.

The frenzy continued. I whirled, ducked, side-stepped, lunged. I slashed, hacked, and parried. The world shrank down to a red-hazed circle, its borders the length of my sword's reach. My breath came in great wheezing sobs, my ribs ached from spear thrust, missed blocks, and exhaustion. I saw through a haze of sweat, blood, and fatigue.

As I slowed, so did the attacks. I realized that many of my attackers were down now, with legs hacked off, or were attacking by lunging and butting, now lacking arms to hold weapons. A welter of severed body parts lay at my feet—arms, hands, legs, heads, and other less easily identified chunks of decaying flesh.

The last two stumbled toward me, one missing both arms, the other limping on a nearly severed leg. They collided, and in their tangle I found the opening for three drawing slashes that left their dismembered parts tangled on the ground.

I stood for a moment, panting, dripping blood. Unusual; all of the blood was mine. Gradually my awareness expanded and my breathing slowed.

"Oh, well done!" Her voiced dripped venom. "I shall have to make more servants when next we meet." I raised my head to see her whip her left arm over her head, dislodging the small black vulture, who flapped his wings twice and began to grow. In a heartbeat he was the size of a pig. In two, larger than a man.

I summoned the dregs of my strength, leapt forward, and struck off his head.

Ananth stumbled back, stunned by the loss of her sorcerous mount. I raised my sword and stalked toward her. She lifted her hand, made a sound that started as a moan and rose in pitch and volume to an ear-shattering shriek. Specks of darkness danced around her like black sparks rising from a fuliginous fire.

And that was all that happened.

"The tooth," I explained. "The Manthycore's talisman. I am guarded from all sorcery, save his."

She stood for a moment gaping, then turned to flee.

I caught her in two steps.

The mare would live. I thought for a time that her heart had burst. But after I cut her hobbles to use as binding cords, she struggled up and stood, sides heaving, eyes rolling, but quite alive. She would need to be rubbed down again. Her sweat made dark streaks in the dust that covered her sides.

The hacked-apart caravan men I stacked just outside the light from the fire. I doubted they would be disturbed, at least not that night and perhaps ever. Their decayed forms reeked even further of the sorcery that had briefly re-animated them.

There was a little water still in my water-skin. I gulped some and used a little of what remained to wash my face and hands. The rest would have to wait until the next oasis.

I turned to the trussed figure that lay on the ground next to the fire. "We will wait for daylight, I think. There is less chance then for you to perform some mischief."

She glared at me from the ground, her raven hair matted and her fine wool wrapping twisted into strips and lumps. I had used some of them to tie her at first, until I could cut the mare's hobbles.

"I am Death, you know," she said. "I cannot be slain!" Her statement would have been bolder if not mumbled through split lips and if her voice had not quavered as she said it.

"You may be right," I conceded.

I looked at her with something akin to affection. She had brought hope with her as a weapon. I had felt its joyous sting. Some still remained, though I think she had not regarded the possibility.

She would have made a treacherous, unreliable ally. She might very well make a pleasing gift.

"I am right. I cannot be slain!"

"Yes, yes. But I think perhaps that will not matter. It may not be possible to slay you." The sun was rising. It was time to see what this last hope might bring. I absently stepped a little to one side to crush a small black serpent under my heel.

"Not slain. But perhaps you may be eaten, anyway."

I drew the talisman from where it rested on my breast, and cleared my thoughts to call the Manthycore.

Not Your Prophesy

Love is the Slayer

He would run away for a few steps, but never far enough that the lion could get its massive body up to speed. Then he would turn, leap back and use his stick to vault over the confused beast, usually whacking it on the head as he passed. He was inhumanly fast and the lion was already lathered and panting. I lowered my bow.

The lion's roars grew fainter as it tired. The young man whirled again, kicking dust up as he spun and dove across the lion's flank. A massive paw swiped at him. Claws scraped against the ragged leather cape that covered its foe's back but the angle was wrong. Instead of raking and shredding, it pushed and both the lion and his enemy fell.

They scrambled in the dust, and for a moment I was convinced that the foolish young man was now the lion's dinner. Odd grunting sounds came through the dust and late-afternoon haze. I slid to the left on my perch, fascinated.

They tumbled onto a patch of gray-green grass, both lion and man streaked with dust, sweat and blood. The man was atop the beast, his stick bowing as he heaved against both ends, its middle across the lion's throat. The lion coughed and twisted, clawed and tumbled. Its spins got progressively slower, its claws at the man on its back sliding harmlessly off his thick leather cape. The lion's struggles grew weaker. It coughed, heaved, rolled on its back in a last attempt to dislodge its tormentor. Slowly it rolled, massive paws clawed at the dust, then was still.

For many heartbeats, the meadow was quiet. Even the wind was silent. I sat down on the rock I had been standing on and waited.

After a few moments the shoulder of the lion rose then fell back. From underneath issued a string of curses, not very imaginative but strong with sincerity. One bare arm reached up and around to haul against the lion's mane. Though thinner than the manes of its cousins in the land of the Nubians, it still provided grip enough for the lion's slayer to heave himself out as far as his waist. He bent over its neck and panted, slowly regaining control of his breath. After awhile he raised his head and spied me watching him. He grinned brightly through the dust and blood that streaked his clean-shaven face.

"Ho, then!" he cried. "What did you see?" He seemed to be no more than twenty summers. His thick black hair streamed in curls about his face, no longer restrained by the torn headband that hung from one end over his ear.

"I saw a fool fight a lion with a stick. The lion seems to have fallen over its own feet and died."

He bellowed a laugh that ended in a cough. He spat blood and a tooth into the dust. "The stick started as a spear but the lion decided that was unfair and so bit the point off."

He pushed at the lion's corpse, heaved himself a little further from under its weight. "So if asked you could stand witness, at least to any who would take the word of a woman."

"Why would any ask? Did not Gilgamesh himself wrestle a lion and win? What one man can do, so can another. Who ever would doubt you?" I asked dryly.

He laughed again. "On reflection, I think I will not ask you to stand witness. When the Oracle's tasks are complete it will not matter that any know what I have done, save by my word. When I am king none will doubt me."

I shook my head and reached to the water skin that hung at my waist. "Here," I said, striding forward. "Drink. It may clear your thoughts, though how clear the thoughts are of one who hunts lions with a stick is a question unanswered."

He reached gratefully for the skin and emptied it in a series of long gasping gulps. He handed it back to me and smiled his thanks. "I am yet a little fatigued and have lost some blood. You are small, but not as old as I first thought. Perhaps with your help I can get from under this beast and so tend my wounds."

I picked up the end of the spear haft that he had used to strangle the lion and tugged it free from under the lion's head. I placed one end under the lion's shoulder and prised at it, beside where the young man's thickly muscled upper body protruded from beneath. With a grunt and a small moan, the man heaved himself free and slid back in the dust. He rested his back against a fallen tree and panted again. Though he was bleeding from more than a half-twelve of places, none of his wounds seemed serious.

"I am Jermaish. I will be king, you know. My uncle is Ashkish, king of the city of Ikizepe, which holds a mountain pass to the north. I will kill him someday, as he killed my father. It will not be easy as he is a great warrior. Many say he is the greatest of our age. He wields a great hammer, so heavy that few men can lift it and none other, even one as strong as I, can use it." His was a wrestler's body, long heavy arms attached to a thick torso, his legs like pillars.

"The greatest warrior of our age." I repeated. What kind of man could inspire such a statement from this mighty young fool?

"I know who you are," he announced. "The Oracle told me to expect you, though I imagined that you would be more comely. After I clean up a bit in yonder stream and bind a scratch or two, you will be my guest at meat and I will tell you my story. I have never before eaten roast lion. It will be a treat."

I too had never before tasted lion. It had a strong, wild flavor, naturally salty, accented wonderfully by the handful of leeks Jermaish found by the stream as he bound his wounds. I seldom notice what I eat, but this was very good.

Jermaish clearly noticed what he ate. He grunted and sighed, clucked in delight and made small noises of pleasure interspersed with heroic belches. He would finish one massive chunk of meat, toss the bone aside and rise to the fire to carve another.

Behind him at the edge of our camp the lion's hide was stretched out to dry, pegged down by rocks. Jermaish had made a paste of the lion's brains and several of its organs and rubbed it into the reverse of the hide to start the tanning process. He would need a cloak to replace the one mauled in the fight.

Finally Jermaish slowed, his belly distended and smeared with grease. He gave a last satisfied belch and started to speak.

"I was born one of many sons of my mighty father, the great Matkish, king of Ikizepe, one of the fifty Cities of the North. I was raised by nurses. I was told by them that my mother had died birthing me. I drew little attention to myself until my teens, when my prowess as a wrestler and as a lover caused many in my city to recall my father in his youth. A few winters ago that idyllic time was cut short by the treachery of my uncle, who murdered my father in his sleep and put to death many of his sons. I was in the arms of a lover that night, and not in the palace. Warned by a servant girl who could not forget the pleasure I had given her just a few nights before, I made my escape. I have wandered these lands, going from city to city, making my coin by wrestling any who will.

"This would be a quite ordinary story, save for two things. One is that I never lose. Not since Gilgamesh himself has there ever been a wrestler such as I am. As a child, one of my nursemaids had whispered to me that my mother did not die in childbirth but instead was a goddess, who had loved my father and had left their issue behind so as not to anger her divine husband. I gave this little thought, thinking that my prowess was due to the strenuous life I led traveling from city to city, and perhaps a patrimony from my great father's loins.

"But a few months ago a strange thing happened. At a caravansary on the road from Nineveh I met an old woman, who had with her a girl who could see things, an oracle. Out of curiosity I gave her a few coins and she took me into her tent, where she fed the girl a draught of some sort and spent several minutes chanting some nonsense in an outlandish tongue that I had never heard before, full of barks and clicks. I was about to leave and seek female companionship of a more amenable sort when the girl screamed, and started reciting. She cried out *'Son of Goddess, Son of King,'* which you must know arrested my departure, as for many years I had told no one of my father and other than a few childish questions of the nurse from my childhood had never spoken of my mother being a goddess.

"She rattled on in screeches and moans, about how I had three tasks to become king, of three trials during my reign and of how I would meet my end, slain by the greatest of all slayers of men. Then she stood straight up, as tall as her half-starved little frame could hold her and screeched a wordless cry that I shall never forget, as if her soul was being ripped from her body with tongs of fire. It was a dreadful sight and for the first time in my life I felt fear, genuine fear, for what is courage, or honor, or strength of arm in the face of the mouthpiece of the gods? Her hair streamed in patches from her head, her eyes bulged sightless and the sores on her face and body glowed brightly against the dirt of her pale, scabby skin. She screamed and screamed, for what seemed a lifetime, which indeed it was, for when she finally stopped to draw breath she shuddered and dropped over, dead before she hit the ground."

He paused to wipe grease from his chin, and to belch reflectively. "I mastered my fear, only to find the old woman cowering in the corner of her tent. I tried a few comforting words, which seemed to help, as she rose and trembling held out the few coins I had given her, groveling all the while. I did not take them back, but instead bade her try and remember what her charge had said, as the fear and shock had driven the details from my mind. She gave me this mnemosyne, this reminder." He pulled from his pouch a small piece of bone, carved into the shape of a broken tooth.

The world spun down, and my mind centered on the small thing he held up for me to see. There was a ringing in my ears, and all the fear and despair of my centuries of servitude came over me. Many lifetimes ago, I had first beheld the original of that talisman. My lover and I had set out to enslave the beast it had come from but instead had been overcome. The sad slow years passed and the talisman that summoned the Manthycore preserved my life and kept me from aging grew heavier and heavier, weighted down with the knowledge of the centuries of murder and betrayal.

I looked down, blinking away the tears that filled my eyes.

"See, I knew that you were the one foretold," he said. "When I saw the talisman you wear about your neck. This one was carved in its likeness. You are the Weeping Betrayer, the servant of the Manthycore. The camel drivers sing of you." Then he raised his voice in a soft, gentle tenor, and sang a verse of the song that through the centuries I have so grown to hate.

Love is the slayer, love the betrayer
Love the blood drinker, slayer of men.
Freedom she seeks, from the binder of youth,
Freedom she seeks, so then binds men in death.

It wasn't much of a city. From Jermaish's description I had expected more. No towering Ur, this was a collection of mud brick houses, brothels, temples and markets surrounded by tumble-down walls. Two guards diced by the River Road Gate, pausing only to make leering catcalls at every sway of hips that passed through. They did not catcall me, though my body is still young. They ignored my companion, hunched over and cloaked.

We found a stable near the palace where for a few small coins they would let us sleep in an unused stall. It was best to keep Jermaish out of sight for the time being, and it served my purpose to leave him in the stall while I ventured out in search of audience with King Ashkish. The closer we got to this city, the more fearsome his reputation was. This made me tend to believe the tales, as usually the prowess of warriors grows as the distance in time and space from their actual feats grows.

I returned several hours later, tired and angry. I had gotten no closer to the king than the outer courtyard, where some instinct of his guards had caused them to make me wait. When finally asked my business they had looked at my scarred and weathered face, listened to my request to see the mighty king who had bested all challengers, measured my small stature, and decided me to be a madwoman. I was shown out politely and the guard who led me to the door pressed a few coins in my palm as he left me.

I spent them and some of my own on a pair of roasted ducks, a pot of boiled barley and a jar of beer. Jermaish ate the bulk of the food while I stewed over a plan. Nothing good presented itself, and I was afraid that Jermaish's disguise hadn't held. I had brought him in the hope he might be useful, though I couldn't see how. What I had come to do had to be done soon, before we were discovered for what we were.

In spite of the words of any oracle, I was not here to aid in Jermaish's ascension to the throne. I was here to meet the man described as the greatest fighter of his age. To kill him if I could, to die if I could not.

"I will go after dark to scout out the palace," I said finally. "The years have taught me stealth, and his palace has low walls. I will be over them before the moon rises. We will see where he sleeps, and if there are any available back ways that leave him vulnerable."

"And then I will slay him," Jermaish insisted.

"Yes," I lied. "Wait here, and when we know more we will lay our plans."

"Not that easy, assassin." The voice rasped from the pillowed alcove ahead. I was deep in the palace, my silent tread and small stature keeping me from discovery. Until now. From the shadows on each side appeared a man. A third stepped into the moonlight that pooled from the smoke-hole in the roof that provided outlet to the circular fireplace in front of the bed.

The man in front of me hefted his spear. A flash from the embers in the fireplace glimmered off of the boss of his round shield. He peered forward, then grunted. "Here, now," he announced, laughter in his voice. "It is the madwoman we told the king about. Come to kill him, then, or perhaps just wishing to share his bed? Either way, you are without luck tonight, I fear. Tonight the king is giving pleasure to the wife of a merchant who displeased him, in the merchant's own bed. Knowing the king, he will not be back before dawn." All three laughed.

I nodded. "Tell me then where he visits and if he carries his hammer with him."

The spearman chuckled. "For the battle he joins tonight he needs only the great hammer between his legs. As to where, I cannot think of a reason why I would tell you."

"Tell me and I won't kill you."

His smile flashed white in his dark beard. "Ahhh, sweetling," he purred. "You'll not kill me if I don't." He leapt over the fireplace, shield clattering against the haft of his spear as he landed, set his feet and thrust true and hard to the center of my chest.

But I was no longer there. I was already at his spear hand side. I sliced down across his throat as I spun behind him. He stumbled forward, gurgling. I pushed him forward with my foot in the small of his back and he fell and skidded on his face across the floor made slick by the spray of his blood.

I whirled to the left. My sword flicked out. The warrior on that side charged into it. He stopped, eyes widening and glazing, the end of his shout dying in his beard. He slid off the bronze point of my sword and folded forward into a bloody heap, his sickle-sword clattering to the ground.

A footstep whispered behind me. I dove forward. As I did, the sweep of an axe yanked at my tunic, just above where my kidneys would have been. I stumbled over the corpse at my feet, landing badly. I scrambled up, barely raising my sword enough to deflect the axe man's second, backhanded blow. My sword rang like an old tired bell, and broke, a jagged half span from its heavy point. I dropped back to one knee and thrust upward under the bronze leaves of his armor, jamming the broken sword up under his ribcage to its hilt. I left it in his corpse, only the oilwood handle visible above the tangle of his armor.

With my boot knife I cut a strip from his thin linen trousers and pressed it against my cheekbone where the flying shard of my sword had laid it open. My back throbbed. I reached back and groped to determine as best I could the extent of the wound. Though my hand came away bloody, it did not seem to be deep. The axe man had not missed me entirely, then.

I stirred the fire with the point of the sickle-sword. It flared up and its light revealed the great hammer where it leaned in a corner by the bed. The sickle sword felt awkward in my hand, lighter and less balanced than the sword I had carried for a dozen or more lifetimes of men. I tossed it aside and picked up instead the spear and shield that lay outstretched beside the corpse of their former owner.

I pulled out the broken tooth talisman that hung around my neck, then hesitated. The Great Beast I served had not fed for many weeks. Soon the Manthycore's desire for the flesh of men would be unbearable, and would haunt me both sleeping and awake. These three would appease it for awhile. But if this king were truly the great warrior all said him to be, it may be that I would be free tonight, slain by him. Then he might be able to slay the Manthycore in turn and so free the one whom I have loved these hundreds of years, preserved unaging by the sorcerous beast.

Slowly I returned the talisman to its resting place. Hope was an infrequent guest and I would not turn it away. I would either die this night or find the Beast meat another time. I moved toward the hammer.

"Psst!" I whirled to the sound, brought my spear point to eye level. From the shadows came Jermaish, finger to lips. "Good that I followed," he whispered.

"There was a fourth guard, who would have raised an alarm. I broke his neck."

For a moment all hung in the balance. I was of a mind to kill him, as his usefulness had passed. But he had been a good companion, full of joy and innocence and he had brightened the journey to his city. His faults were those of an overgrown dog, bumbling and overeager and the only times he had annoyed me were when he sang the caravan song about me, delighted to know someone in a song, and the several times I had been awakened by the ghosts of my dreams, the long parade of faces of murdered men. Each time he had generously offered to allow me to share his bed, as everyone knew that the best cure for night fears was a good rogering. Though I was not at all comely, still I was a woman, with a woman's weakness of need. I finally shut him up by telling him that the centuries of disuse had caused my lotus to heal over, eliminating that womanly weakness.

I sighed. "Bring the hammer. I'll explain when we get there." He hefted it over his shoulder. The haft was a man's length, with a head the size of an ox's. It was made of some fire-hardened wood, with bronze nails and straps to add weight and strength. I am certain that I could not have carried it, at least for any distance.

"Where do we go?"

"To wherever we see lights. The king is unlikely to go to his assignation quietly, not if it is to punish one of his subjects. He will have taken servants and guards. There will be many torches and lanterns. All we must do is look to the night sky."

I had spent more time sneaking around in the dark tonight than I had done for decades. For such a large man, Jermaish was remarkably light on his feet and so was far less of a liability than I had feared. We found where the King was spending the night with little trouble. There were less than a dozen, those few nodding off in the narrow street in front of the house as the moon came near to setting. The grounds were walled, but even though the bricks of the wall had been recently plastered to make them smooth, there were still enough handholds available, especially after Jermaish used the butt of the hammer, wrapped in his shirt, to make a few new ones. Over we went and into the unfortunate merchant's garden. It was the work of a moment to find the right window; light from dozens of candles leaked through its shutter and a regular rhythmic moaning came from within. I motioned to the next window over and we crawled silently in, finding ourselves in an opulent bath in the style of the lands of the Two Kingdoms. A closed door was all that separated us from the room which held the king.

"Put the hammer against the wall there by the door," I hissed. "And then look out the window, and see if we are discovered." He leaned the massive hammer against the wall and turned to peer out the small window we had come through. I rapped him sharply across the temple with the butt of my spear, then caught him best as I could as he fell bonelessly straight down. I laid him out on the mosaic floor. He immediately started a soft snoring, so I was reasonably certain I hadn't killed him.

Silently I opened the door and lifted the hammer through to set it inside the room in which the king was enjoying his revenge. I bolted the door, then crossed through the candlelight to the room's other door and let drop the bar.

The activity on the bed stopped and a giant's head lifted from the blankets. "I said I wanted nothing more. Leave me!" he growled.

"It is not your desire I am here to serve, O King."

He snorted and pushed away from the pale figure beneath him. The blanket flew back to reveal the naked form of a frail-looking woman, the kohl beneath her eyes running and smeared with tears.

"What is this?"

"I have come to kill you, Ashkish of Ikizepe."

"Are you an assassin, then?" He rose naked to his full height. He was truly a giant, standing half again as tall as a normal man, hugely muscled. "Why, you are an ill-grown assassin, then. Come closer, so I may strangle you."

"I will not, O King. I have brought your great hammer, which you may wield. There is much room here and light enough that we may fight."

He peered closer. "Why, you are that madwoman who bothered my gatekeepers earlier today. It made for an amusing story. Very well, then. As you have gone to such great trouble to die, I shall oblige you." He edged over to where his hammer rested against the wall near the door to the bath.

He was deadly fast. The hammer came up in a blur, seeming to leap into his hand. It spun in his grasp like the lightest of twigs, humming through the air at blinding speed. I was faster, of course, simply by virtue of my size, but I knew in the first few instants that I had never met his like, and my heart leapt with joy and real hope. The hammer buzzed over my head, whipping my braid away with the force of its passage and then was as quickly back, forcing me to leap away. I licked in, thrust into his thigh and he bellowed, then missed taking my head off by a hair's breadth as he wheeled the hammer back over his shoulder. It caught the edge of my shield and ripped it away, breaking its straps and hurling it against the far wall, knocking over on its way a table of guttering candles. I felt my fingers break as it left my grasp and the broken strap slice into my forearm, but there was no time to heed the pain, sharp though it was.

He grinned through his curled and oiled beard and stepped forward, bringing the hammer over his head. He misjudged the ceiling and clipped a beam. His belly was open and I lunged with my spear, both hands on the haft, and thrust with all the strength and speed my centuries of fighting had gained me.

Impossibly he spun to my right and instead of opening his belly, the point of my spear ripped into his arm and on up his shoulder. Blood sprayed and he stumbled back. I moved to the kill, spear high to thrust down through his collarbone and leapt up. He swatted me out of the air like a fly, the backhand of his hammer enough to numb my hip and send me crashing against the barred door, breath knocked out of my lungs.

I struggled up, much slower than I wanted. He was losing blood and I could see by his new caution that he had learned to respect my skill. If I could hold him for even a few more moments, he would be weak enough that I could overcome him. Even giants cannot lose too much blood. I tasted the ashes of despair. If this man could not slay me, then who ever could?

Slowly I circled him where he stood panting, waiting for the hammer to waver. In truth, the slow was not caution. I was having trouble where the hammer had hit my hip. I did not think it was broken, but it was rapidly failing.

"That's all?" he taunted. The blood from his leg wound and the rip in his shoulder pattered down, black in the uncertain candlelight. He raised the hammer and I darted in.

The world exploded. I was against the wall, and I couldn't breathe. My chest made a gurgling sound each time I tried and my right side screamed with pain. I tried to cry out, but had no air to do so.

There was a throbbing sound in my ears, like a distant drum. Dimly, I realized that it was my heartbeat, slow and irregular. There were hazy lights in the distance, blurred and flickering like stars under a light haze. They were obscured by the black-haired face of a giant. The king, I realized.

"The talisman," I gasped, or tried to. "Take it."

He grunted and I felt a jolt that turned everything into dark, whirling spots. Perhaps he kicked me. I no longer cared, as the swelling joy of my freedom in death lifted me out and into the waiting darkness. I was free!

I was standing in an orchard, awash in a sea of spring blossom. Holding my hand was a small child, a girl of five or six summers. She was ragged but clean, skinny but glowing in health.

"Am I dead then?" I asked. She didn't answer, but instead led me to the road I knew lay just beyond the trees. I looked down to find myself standing in tall grass, the white of my tunic bright against the rich green. The girl tugged against my hand, and I saw that my skin was milky, smooth, unscarred. She led me to the center of the road, where there was a small leather pack propped against a stone. She gestured me to open it, so I did. Inside was a leather strap, knotted to hold a large broken tooth, jagged and stained. It meant something, I knew, but I couldn't remember.

"It wasn't your prophecy," she whispered from behind me. "Your tale is for another time." The warm sun brightened and brightened and I tumbled into the growing light.

If there was someplace I didn't hurt, it was unimportant. I woke in pain and for a while I swam in it, sometimes hearing voices, sometimes not. Night and day were random between blinks and time seemed to mean nothing. After what I knew to be a long while I awoke and knew who I was. "I am king now," said a voice. I turned my head as best I could to find Jermaish beside me. Bitterness welled up and I smothered a sob. He wavered in my sight, from pain and tears. "I will kill you," I whispered.

He smiled. "You are welcome. And I am grateful, which is a great virtue in a king, I am told. Had you not weakened him I could not have overpowered him when he came to wash and bind his wounds. In the end it came down to wrestling and even he could not stand before me then."

"You stole my death," I whispered. "I am still enslaved."

"You are still alive. I nursed you with my own hands. You should have died, you know. Any other mortal would have, or so my healers tell me. This talisman of yours is a fearsome thing, is it not? It has amazing healing properties. Ashkish crushed your chest. It was caved in, and bones stuck out. Your hip was broken and your wrist and fingers, too. But you are whole now and soon you will be able to walk and to travel.

"The scholars tell me of a wise man, in a city far to the south along the Euphrates. This man knows all the ways of beasts and plants, great and small. He may have knowledge of the beast you serve and how to be free from it. You will go there when you are able. I am king now and cannot harbor one as murderous as you in my kingdom."

I coughed and he reached across me to a table on the other side of the bower I lay in to produce a cup. He held it to my lips and I drank. It was cool, water mixed with sweet wine. "By the way, I looked when I nursed your wounds. It is not healed over from disuse. You are a woman whole."

I glared at his face, wishing I had strength enough to strangle him.

He plucked a date from the bowl at his elbow, looked it over, then held it to my mouth. I nibbled, then took it whole, suddenly ravenous.

"I had your sword remade while you slept, and new clothes prepared."

"I will kill you with it. You betrayed me."

"No you won't. The Oracle told me how I would die, remember? I will be struck down by the greatest of all slayers of men."

I laughed bitterly. It hurt. "Who has murdered more than I? And now it will continue."

He smiled and patted my cheek. I didn't bite him, though I wished to. "Why time, of course. And no matter how long you live, you too will be time's fool, in the end."

As he rose to leave I caught a glimpse of a small talisman, carved of bone in the shape of a broken tooth, white and clean where it rested on a chain against the black of the hair of his chest.

Wasted Words

Weaving Spiders Come Not Here

The prow of the stitched reed boat pushed into the mud of the riverbank and we came to a stop. The tattered red sail was clumsily rigged and had propelled us across at less than a walking pace. But we were across, and I stepped out into the brown Euphrates water and waded ashore. Behind me, the other passengers splashed their way to dry land. I ignored them, as I had ignored them the night before as we camped at the caravansary, waiting for daylight and the ferry across.

They were slave traders and their goods. Being a slave myself, though to no man, I have an aversion to slave traders. No doubt, seeing a woman traveling by herself, they had weighed the possibility of adding me to their inventory but I am no longer comely. The scars of countless battles across 40 lifetimes of men are etched into my face and though I have not aged, the bitterness of my servitude has burned away any sweetness of youth I may have once had.

The thickness of my wrist where it rested across the well-worn oilwood hilt of my sword may have influenced them as well. Slave traders are cowards. There is easy prey all around them and little profit to be had from quarry that fights back.

Pity.

The reed-lined mud bank sloped up to a cut made by the feet of generations of ferrymen and their passengers. At each side were huts made of the same stitched and bundled reeds that the ferry was made of. A dog and several small naked children played beneath the hulk of its predecessor where it lay rotting on the bank.

I walked up to the crest of the bank. A handful of discouraged trees and a bedraggled garden baked there. I was almost to the road beyond when voices cried out behind me. I turned and watched as a small girl, perhaps eight or ten summers old, broke free from the handful of slaves being led up the hill behind me. One of the slavers loped after her.

She ran up the bank, straight toward me. Her black hair flopped in strings past her shoulders where it blended into the black cotton of her shift. She seemed to my eyes to be from the land east of the Great Northbound River that strung together the Two Kingdoms. Many slaves came to the cities of the plain from there. The Pharaohs like their wars and make poor neighbors.

Her pursuer caught her just before she reached me. She ducked, slipped his grasp and ran up, grabbed at my hand. I let her.

"You are the woman from the song!" she cried.

I didn't answer.

"I prayed for you to come." The slave trader reached out to grab her by the hair. I batted his hand away, not looking. He growled through brown stained teeth, reached for a knife at his waist, thought better of it.

I pulled my hand from hers, shook my head. "You wasted your breath, child."

I turned back to the road.

"And yet here you are!" she cried behind me. She was silenced by a slap.

"And yet here I am," I whispered. I frowned up at the morning sun. Soon it would be intolerably hot and it was at least a fifth of a day's walk to the gates of the city I planned to visit. A companion would make it take longer but then again, if they have taken so much, in return the endless long years have given me patience.

I turned and called after the trader, who was pushing the girl ahead of him by one arm. "How much?"

He stopped and glared over his shoulder. "For this one?"

"Yes." This is any merchant's favorite word and his frown changed into an unctuous smile. We haggled for a bit, reached an agreement. He went down the bank happy and I turned once again to the road, this time with the child behind me.

I surprised myself, which happens with vanishing rarity. Why had I purchased the girl? Certainly I was purchasing no redemption. I have done so much murder through the centuries that buying and freeing one little girl wasn't going to atone for even the smallest measure. It couldn't have been sympathy. I have walked past thousands of slaves without feeling much more than mild pity. Innocence might have moved me, were I capable of being moved, but my own was so far in the past as to no longer be even a memory.

I no longer believed in gods, except perhaps one and Him I could not embrace. He reserved vengeance to Himself. Long after hope had vanished, the desire for revenge on the beast that held me in service still burned. Yet she prayed for me to come, and here I was. Most likely it was mere chance.

After all these years it is inevitable that I occasionally be recognized, though I travel widely to avoid it. Sometimes it is an old mother who remembers me through blurry eyes and the fog of years between her dotage and her childhood as the one who lured away her father or uncles. Or through rare carelessness on my part, I am seen too soon passing through a city where in the recent past I have plied my trade. And yes, once in a great while I am recognized from that cursed song, loved far too well by travelers throughout the heart of the world.

I hate that song. It is a good song, haunting and strange. The tale it tells is irresistible, about a boy and a maid, a fell beast, a great treasure, and a mistress of death who leads men to their dooms. In the song the boy saves the maid, slays the beast, outwits the betrayer, and wins the treasure:

What has been destroyed belongs now to no one.
No one is able to take it away.
What will be destroyed belongs to the Servant
Who comes for the mother's fruit and takes it away.
She is a destroyer, a slayer of men.
Men who would do ill, men who have done ill,
But justice does not broaden her breast
Neither does vengeance, though claim it she may.
Love is the slayer, love the betrayer
Love the blood drinker, slayer of men.
Freedom she seeks, from the binder of youth,
Freedom she seeks, so then binds men in death.

Songs all end right. Life does not.

I reached the road. Behind me light steps told me that the girl followed.

"Wait," she gasped. I didn't answer.

Her steps quickened, and soon she was panting beside me.

"Where are we going?" she asked.

"Ashkesht. The city ahead."

"Is it then a great city?"

"No." In fact it could only be considered a city by nature of its location on the great road, the fact that it was walled in crumbling mud brick, and that it had a prince as its ruler who owed allegiance but not servitude to Ur, which lay a mere five days march away. There are larger villages in the world than Ashkesht.

It had one other thing, though, which brought me to it. A wise man dwelt there, one renowned even in his own lifetime for his knowledge of beasts and plants and men. A wise man who might tell me of a way to be free of the bitter servitude of the centuries.

"Will we eat there?"

I looked down at her. Her face was thin. Her previous owner had not looked terribly prosperous. Most likely the slaves were fed only enough to keep them alive, to get them to market.

I fumbled in the bag that hung from my shoulder, found a crust left from my meal the night before. She grabbed it, and began gnawing at it with an urgency that told me that whatever she had been before, recently she was ill-fed.

As we walked the dusty road, dodging the occasional slow moving farm wagons, I considered her and the odd impulse that caused me to buy her. It bothered me in ways I couldn't entirely explain to myself. What was she, to me? And what was I to do with her? I had no need for a servant, even less for a pet. If I turned her loose she would starve. If I sold her to someone else she would most likely end her life in a brothel.

When the last nibble of the crust was gone, she began humming the song again:

Bright shines the treasures dreamed of by youth.
Companions and lovers they journey their way.
The great beast ahead will serve them compelled
By the talisman given on a road stretched behind.
Many years passed now the Betrayer has saved them.

Many years passed — since the beast was destroyed.
Many years passed now — the Betrayer still wanders.
Many years passed — but the slayer still slays.
Many lives passed now — the Betrayer has slain them.
Many lives passed — under heavy-tipped sword.
Many lives passed now — to feed the enslaver.
Many lives past — since enslaver was slain.

Another question snaked its way into my thoughts.

"You say you prayed that I would come?"

"And you did!" she exclaimed around a mouthful of bread.

"Why?"

"I wanted to you to kill them all."

There was no answer to this. It was not innocence, then, that had drawn me.

We walked in silence until we reached the gates.

They were unguarded, of course. They had not been closed, by the look of them, since before the birth of the child who walked beside me. The walls they hung from were in disrepair, broken mud bricks fallen from the walls above making small slopes up their sides. Occasional small plants grew from between the brick courses, breaking the dusty red-brown with splashes of tired green.

The city stank, as all cities do. There was no pretense of order; houses, shops and taverns huddled together, sharing walls and patrons. The filth-strewn streets were no more than the habit-traveled paths between buildings. There was an occasional well surrounded by trampled mud. I knew that there was a temple somewhere near the center and there must have been a palace of some sort, perhaps as part of the temple, but I could not recall.

It was not a busy place. I asked directions at every opportunity, but it still took us several false turns and backtracks from dead ends before we finally found ourselves in front of a rare walled house, fancier than any around it but in the same state of disrepair. A red symbol I didn't recognize was painted on the wall near the door. It looked like a fist holding a handful of twigs. The door was ajar. I pushed it open and we went through into the courtyard beyond.

It was cleaner there, though still not neat. Weeds grew up between the cobbles and we had to circle a dry fountain to reach the door of the house. To one side were fallen-down empty stables; to the other a dusty vegetable garden.

I pounded on the dark wooden door. There was a wait and then it heaved open. On the other side stood an old, bent man, blinking through rheumy eyes at the brightness of the day.

"You are not the man with the chickens!" he accused.

"I am not," I agreed.

"Then why are you here?"

"To speak with the master of the house."

He grunted and motioned us in, closed the door behind us.

"What do you want?" Now it was our turn to be blinded. The room was dark, lit by a smoke hole in its center. Against the pillar of light it admitted the size and shape of the room was hard to judge, shadowed but seeming large.

"As I said, the master of the house."

"Speak, then," he snapped. "As I am he and have no time for fools."

I cleared my throat. "I wish for knowledge," I said. "I wish to learn of the Manthycore.

He barked a laugh. "Treasure seeker or glory seeker? Or most likely both."

"Neither. I wish to slay it and so be free."

He stopped mid-cackle. In the gloom I could see him lean forward, peer at me.

"Follow," he commanded, in a firmer voice than before. He led us into another room, better lit by light that streamed in through open windows. On a table in the center were the partially dismembered remains of a dog. On shelves lining the room were hundreds of small clay jars. To one side was a second table with clay frame, water ewer and stylus ready to make the small tablets used to record events and send messages between courts and temples.

"Let me look at you." He led me into the light and peered at me. After a moment I realized he was chanting something under his breath. The broken tooth talisman that rested on a chain around my neck stirred and then quieted.

"It is you!" he exclaimed. "I thought you to be only a part of the story."

"I am."

"Yes, yes, but you are also a woman, not just words in a tale." He hummed to himself for a bit. The talisman did nothing, so humming was all it was. He looked over to the girl, dismissed her as unimportant. "We will trade," he said finally. "Tell me your tale and I will tell you what I know. Your servant can fetch us wine from the ewer by the window."

"Not my servant."

"Daughter, then." I didn't correct him.

A quarter day passed as I told him my story, prompted occasionally by a sharp question. I don't think I had ever told anyone before and it was like a great unburdening. A few times I wept.

I spoke of my earliest days, of growing up the daughter of a minor merchant, of meeting my love, of the day we played in the orchard, glowing in the joy of first love. I told him how we came upon an ambush and with our bows slew the bandits who attacked an old man but could not save him. Before he died, he gave us the talisman I wear around my neck and told us of a great treasure guarded by a foul beast and showed us how to use the talisman to summon it. But the talisman did not control the beast. Lifetimes had passed, and I had spent the years in murder.

From a young fool who fought a lion with a stick I learned of this old man. He was held by many to be wiser in the ways of beasts and men than any other before him back to Utnapishtim, known by some as Noach, to whom was given mastery over all beasts so that he might save them from the deluge. If any could tell me how to free myself and my love, it would be him.

As I spoke, I sipped wine from my cup. I mixed it with water from the ewer and salt from my tears. The old man's occasional question steered my narrative and prodded my memory. Much that was forgotten came to the surface. I am not certain how long I have been in bondage, but in those years the city in which I was born was destroyed by war and another built on its site. There are none who now live there now who even know that the previous city existed. To my sorrow, I realized that I no longer recalled even its name, so that all who dwelt there, lived there, loved there were forgotten as though they never were.

After a while, I fell silent. My ward had listened intently for a great while, but finally she had drowsed and now slept at my feet. The old man sat across from me, blinking and humming, seemingly out of questions.

I brushed the tears from my cheeks and took a long drink of wine. The deep blood red was little diluted by the water I added. It was fittingly bitter.

"Can you then help me?" I asked finally.

He hummed a little, and then spoke. "I can. Perhaps."

He went over to a stack of tablets next to a disorderly box filled with scrolls and codices. From near the bottom he pulled a clay slab scratched over with odd angular marks in lined-out rows. He stared at it for a moment, shook his head, and called for a servant. He whispered to him for a moment in a language I didn't recognize, and the servant hurried out. He returned in a few minutes with another box of scrolls, muttered something in the same strange tongue, and left.

At my feet the girl stirred.

The old man studied a crumbling scroll for a few moments, humming as always. Then he looked up. "Yes, yes. I think it may be done. There are seven herbs, the *Shappatu*, found in the direction of the setting sun near the mountains where man first was made. The writings contained in this scroll tell me that they were cultivated by Adapa, the servant of Enki Himself and have power over all living things. Blended together they will compel obedience of any who consume them, even the great beast whom you serve, who has existed since before life was blown into men of clay."

The girl tugged at the hem of my garment. I waved her away.

"How will I know these herbs?"

"You may ask of any cunning woman or herb doctor. The herbs are well known there, where the great kings of the Khett rule over cities of stone. They are used in love potions and the like." He blinked rapidly and glanced at the door.

"If there is nothing more that you can tell me, we will take our leave. It seems I have many days travel ahead through often hostile lands." I rose, or tried to. I found that my legs would not quite work the way I intended.

My sword was out without my thinking it, and I pushed myself to my feet with the strength of my free arm against the table and sheer will. The old man surprised me with his agility by leaping back and scrambling to put a table between us while crying out an inarticulate warble.

The room clattered full with men.

Hope, unaccustomed hope, had made me a fool. All my years of being the betrayer, and I had let the glimmer of a chance of freedom blind me to his betrayal.

"Forgive me," hissed the old man from the safety of his corner, now masked from me by two armored men as well as the table. "What you carry is too valuable to let slip away."

I took three rapid breaths. The room steadied, and the crowd between me and the door resolved into only four. This with the two in the corner made six.

"I must know," I said. "Was what you told me true? Will these *Shappatu* indeed bind the beast?"

"Yes, but I am afraid it will not be you who does the binding."

"Oh, but it will." They were fools. They could have stood away, and shot me down like a stray dog. But none of them carried bows, only spears.

I leaned forward and groaned. Two moved forward as if to catch me and with two quick strokes I cut them down. I could not move my legs, and I felt as weak as a newborn, but the heavy bronze tip of my sword needed only my guidance and experience. The other two dashed forward. And died.

A line of fire seared across my ribs. I looked down to see a spearhead as it finished its scrape across my body. I turned into it, trapping it under my arm. I lashed out, backhanded, and felt my sword connect with meat and bone. The spearman screamed. His companion leaned forward, spear at ready. I pulled my sword to block his blow, but it stuck, and I hadn't the strength to free it.

The spearman grinned, his teeth flashing in the uncertain light. He started forward, and then stumbled.

The girl threw herself at his knees, wrapping arms and legs around them. I summoned what I had of my strength and gave a great tug, freeing my sword. As I did, he swung his spear around and clubbed her away with such force that she bounced against the table leg and lay still.

He did not get the spearhead around fast enough to stop the blow I aimed at the base of his neck. My aim was poor. I hit him in the jaw. He fell moaning and gurgling to the floor.

"In the water or the wine, old man?"

"The drug was in the wine," he quavered.

"Good." I upended the water ewer, took great gulps. When I was finished I looked over at the girl. She lay in a heap under the table, a small pool of blood under her.

"See if she lives," I commanded.

He hesitated, and then scurried over. He laid her on her back. There was a gash along her scalp, over her right eye, about a finger-length. He bent over her, pushed away her hair and listened at her mouth. "She breathes," he announced after a moment.

"Then so do you."

He reached up to the table, took the ewer and used the remaining water to rinse away the blood. His fingers probed at the wound, seeking further injury. As he did so, she moaned, and her eyes fluttered. She sat up, and I waved him back to his corner. "No broken head," he said.

"Then you keep your hands as well as your life."

He shuddered, started to speak, thought better.

"How long?" I asked.

"The drug? Perhaps an hour, perhaps less. Less I think with you. The sorcery of the talisman will not prevent poisoning, but will restore those who survive it more rapidly. The same goes for mere drugs."

"Good. Rise child, and bring me that spear." Her eyes steadied and focused. She got up slowly and did as I bid her, stumbling over bodies, her tread uncertain in the spilled blood.

I wiped my sword on the tunic of a man who had fallen across the table, then sheathed it. I turned the spear butt-down. It would make a serviceable staff. "Take the old man this wine," I told her. "He will drink it all, and when he sleeps, we will leave.

The fire snapped at the dark, pushing it back from the edge of our camp, which I had made a hundred steps from the western road. As we left Ashkesht I purchased a pot of lentils, onions and herbs. It now sat empty by the fire.

The girl watched me, bright-eyed over the fire as I cleaned the dried blood from my side. "You heal quickly," she said.

"Yes." Something occurred to me. "Have you a name?"

"I am Miri. What is your name?"

I was silent for a long while. The fire crackled, night birds cried, in the brush nearby a small animal scrabbled in the dirt.

When men face betrayal — the Betrayer's sword dampens.
Betrayer of men — yet betrayers she slays.
But justice does not — broaden her breast
Neither does vengeance, — though claim it she may.
Love is the slayer, — love the betrayer,
Love the blood drinker, — slayer of men.
Freedom she seeks, — from the binder of youth,
Freedom she seeks, — so then binds men in death.
Bright shone the treasures — dreamed of by youth.
Companions and lovers — they journeyed their way.
The great beast ahead — would serve them compelled
By the talisman given — on a road stretched behind.

"I don't remember," I said at last.

"That is so sad!" she exclaimed. "I will make a name for you, then. I will call you Nin-Sinnus."

Nin-Sinnus. Lady of the Song.

"Call me what you will," I grunted, but I was pleased. It was a beautiful name, the first beautiful thing about me in more than forty lifetimes of men. I had gained much this day. Hope now walked with me. My bondage and the bondage of my lover perhaps would now perhaps finally end.

A companion walked with me as well. She was underfed, ignorant and no doubt would be a burden every day she traveled with me. I would start her tomorrow learning how to defend herself with staff, bow, sword and spear. By the time we reached the mountains of Khett perhaps she could defend herself.

Lady of the Song. Perhaps this time, I would make the song come true.

Staring Through the Gate

The Tears of Ishtar

Iten

Part One: The Tavern Goddess

Miri knew little about her new mother except what she had gleaned from the caravan songs, and what she had been told in the few months they had traveled together. Now, as they hurried through the crowded dirt streets of Carcamesh, she thought to wonder about her. Had her mother ever really been a girl, as Miri was, amazed and confused by the sights and sounds of a great city like this one which standing near the borders of Khett? Or, as seemed more likely, had she just always been, formed at the beginning of the world to spend the centuries wandering as cities rose and fell, more marvelous herself than any place where dwelt men?

She shifted the heavy pack she carried, and scrambled to catch up. Her mother's thick, oiled braid swung from side to side in counter-point to her firm steps. She was small in stature, not much taller than Miri, who at mid-year would be nine summers old. Still, there was something about her that made people step aside. Twice, from the corner of her eye, Miri saw people make small signs of protection against evil. It made her smile.

"There." Ninshi pointed to a bench in front of a low white-washed building. Over the door hung a sheaf of barley. "We will wait here until dark."

Miri sighed and put down her pack. Her shoulder was sore, but she didn't complain. Her mother seemed deaf to such, anyway. As she sat down she made certain, as she had been taught, that the handle of her knife was clear of the folds of her shift. She saw her mother nod approvingly. It warmed her from inside, and emboldened her.

"Ninshi?" Miri asked. "What is this place?"

Her mother still seemed startled at being called by name, even though it was just the name Miri had given her to replace the one lost to memory. "This is a tavern, child. Men drink here."

"Yes, Ninshi. But why have we traveled to this tavern? I thought we were bound for Khett. Are you thirsty, then?"

Ninshi shook her head. A stray beam of late-afternoon sun glanced across her cheek, washing out the scars. Her face was not old, but it was weathered and marked by lifetimes of grief and despair. "We are for Khett. But first we must ask advice from someone older even than I. Khett is a great land, and we might search for many years and still not find what we seek." She turned her head as she spoke, her glance falling in seeming idleness on two men who lingered amidst the trash piled at the street's end. They had passed them when they paused at the tavern door, perhaps not knowing that the street ended there.

"The Tavern-Keeper dwells here," Ninshi continued, not taking her eye from the idlers, who were now whispering to each other, heads together. "She is the protector of this city, but she also hears all that is said over jug, mug or bowl, at least in any tavern or caravansary where her name is still honored." She stretched and scratched her hip, loosening her sword in its wolf's skin scabbard as she did so.

The move didn't gone unnoticed. The two men straightened and hurried away, nodding as they passed. Under normal circumstances two women alone at twilight in the oldest part of the city would seem easy prey, but not if one of them was well-armed, hard-looking and wary. There were cults who trained women as guards and warriors. Better to seek more toothless quarry.

"Ninshi, what..."

"Quiet now, and listen." She grasped Miri's shoulder. "We have only a moment, for we must cross the threshold as the final beam of sunlight does. You must be silent inside. Speak only if the Tavern-Keeper asks you a question. Answer in truth, for she will know if you do not."

"What if she asks me something I cannot answer?"

"Then tell her so, but be certain that such is the truth. You may never in your life face one so dangerous. Some say she is the Goddess of Drunkards. If so, she is the most eagerly worshipped of all deities and has followers wherever there are men." She looked at the lowering sun, gestured for Miri to rise, and started for the door.

"Is she truly a goddess, then?" asked Miri, snatching up her pack.

Ninshi shook her head. "I do not believe in any gods save one and Him I do not worship." She glanced over her shoulder, nodded, and pushed open the door. "I do believe in power, though." She shoved Miri through and followed.

There was smoke and the smell of sweat, burnt meat and spilt beer. A large fire burned brightly in a fireplace in the center of the room. Oil lamps added light and smoke in the corners, which seemed to be too many for the shape of the room. Save for the two of them, the tavern was empty. Ninshi gestured at a bench and they sat, resting their elbows on the worn planks of a trestle-table.

"There in a moment, dears!" caroled a voice from somewhere in the back. Miri looked about the tavern. There were curious things hung about, many of them hard to see. On the nearest wall was a stretched skin covered with simple figures of animals and men with spears, painted with fading colors. Above them hung a dusty lyre, much like those Miri had seen played far to the south in the Two Kingdoms, where she was born and was sold into slavery with the rest of her people.

"You'll be wanting to ease your thirst, no doubt," said the matronly woman who bustled in. She was wearing an apron over a simple shift, the traditional garb of tavern-keepers. In one hand she carried a large jug; in the other were balanced two deep bowls. She put a bowl in front of each of them, and filled them both with a stream of amber liquid.

Miri looked up. The woman was tall and full-bosomed, but seemed to carry herself lightly, in spite of her size. Her face was lightly wrinkled, her nose reddened by fine veins that wandered across her face to fade away on her cheeks. She smiled down at her, and Miri lowered her head and pretended to study her bowl.

"We have come seeking news, Matar Kubileya, Mistress of the Tavern," began Ninshi.

"News is indeed my second stock in trade," smiled Kubileya. "Gossip, whispered plots, lover's quarrels, tall tales, and lies told to seduce. Traveler's tales, village wisdom, epic poems, idle jests, drunkard's banter. Calumny, dirty linen, a wife's confession of infidelity to her best friend, hearsay, scandal, slander and slime. There is always time for news. But first you will eat." She spun on her heel and was gone, pausing only to flick a crumb from the corner of a table as she passed.

Ninshi shrugged, and picked up her bowl. Miri followed suit. She sipped cautiously at the foamy brew. She didn't care much for beer. Her birth family had drunk millet beer with breakfast every day, and she had once had a sip of the sour pombe brewed by the Nubian slave traders who had transported her around the Middle Sea to the land between the Rivers. This was different. In it she could taste warm summers and gentle autumns, harvests and planting and life as it grew from seed to stalk. She gulped greedily, and felt its coolness spread from her throat to her limbs.

She felt a hand on her shoulder, looked up to see Ninshi shaking her head. For a moment she thought of defying her and drinking even deeper, and then terrified at such a thought, lowered the bowl.

She was saved from her embarrassment by the arrival of Matar Kubileya and their meal. She set a great steaming bowl between them, filled with rice and chunks of meat. For the next several minutes she was busy, rolling the rice into balls and stuffing them into her mouth. The slavers had fed her, but never enough, and the weeks since Ninshi had bought her from them had not been enough to break her habit of hunger. The meat was highly spiced, savory with fat and juices. She wasn't certain, but thought it might be young camel.

The bowl was nearly empty before she was finished. Miri wiped her greasy mouth with her hand, and then wiped her hand on her shift. Being not hungry was good, she decided, and leaned back to pat her contentedly bulging belly. Ninshi and Matar Kubileya were already talking.

"...I know of this," nodded Kubileya. "Several weeks ago, an old man wept over his wine of a lost talisman that would have given him many lifetimes for study."

Ninshi smiled her grim half-smile. It was more a baring of teeth than an expression of goodwill. "I think the price would have been higher than he thought, those extra years, with little time for learning."

"May I see it?" asked Kubileya.

Ninshi nodded, and pulled the leather thong which hung about her neck, revealing a large broken-tooth talisman, stained darkly. It hung between her fingers, the lamp-light reflecting dully from its irregular surface.

Kubileya leaned forward, her eyes bright with fascination. "The Manthycore's tooth," she breathed. "Such an evil thing, so much blood and death. Is this then by which it is summoned?"

"Yes. Would you like me to show you?"

Kubileya recoiled. "No, no!" she snapped. "I have no wish to be beast fodder. He has eaten others of my kind, as you know."

"Yes," replied Ninshi. "I have seen this."

Kubileya sighed. "Far too dangerous a thing to have about, I think. I would not like for you to decide to dwell for too long in my city."

"None do, and I stay seldom. I have come only to learn of something. This same old man you spoke of told me of seven herbs, called by the ancients the *Shappatu*, found in the direction of the setting sun near the mountains where man first was made. The writings contained in a scroll told him that they were cultivated by Adapa, the servant of Enki Himself. These I wish to find."

The Tavern Goddess smiled. “I can help you with this, my dear. But of course, there is something I need, and it is only fair that if I help you, you help me. Have you time for a story?”

Ninshi nodded.

Kubileya lifted her bowl and drank from it. When she had finished, she set it down and cleared her throat, and began speaking. She spoke of the goddess Ishtar, and her descent into the underworld, on a task whose nature and goal had long been lost to time. The goddess approached the gates of the underworld and demanded that the gatekeeper open them.

“Ishtar, first among goddesses, told the Gatekeeper that unless he let her pass, she would break the door to pieces, and hurl down the gateposts. She would set the dead to eat the living, and soon the dead would outnumber them.

“The gatekeeper relayed this message to Ereshkigal, the Queen of the Underworld. She bade Ishtar enter, but according to the ancient rule she must leave something at each of the seven gates. Now some say this was to be an article of clothing. Others claim it was a body part. Still others claim it was the memory of a lover to be lost at each stop. No one knows, but whatever it was, it caused Ishtar great grief, so much so that at every gate she stopped for a time to weep. Her tears formed a ball in the dust of the Underworld Road.

“By the time Ishtar had reached the throne of Ereshkigal she had fallen into a great rage, and would have destroyed her, but even great Ishtar could not defeat Death herself in her own kingdom. Ereshkigal ordered her servant Namtar to bind Ishtar and to torment her with disease.

"Of course, with the Goddess of Love imprisoned, and perhaps dead, all men found themselves unable to pleasure their wives. There was a great wailing and gnashing of teeth, so great that it rose into the heavens, disturbing the peace and leisure of the gods. Even worse, the gods themselves were so afflicted. Ea, the King of the Gods, sent his servant Asu-shu-namir to Ereshkigal. There he sprinkled Ishtar with the water of life, restoring her and setting her free. Then Ishtar journeyed back through the seven gates, gathering back her clothing or body parts, or the memory of a lover, or whatever it was that she had given as she passed each gate.

"But her tears she left behind. Mixed with the dust of the Underworld Road, they became transformed into rubies, seven perfect and beautiful rubies, one for each gate Ishtar wept at. No one now remembers if Ishtar in fact accomplished the task that led her to descend into that terrible place. But the rubies are remembered."

Kubileya sipped at her beer bowl, and then continued. "The rubies have been fought over and coveted by princes, kings, priests and merchants ever since. Even the gods have sometimes coveted them. Gilgamesh had three of them in his crown. The king of Kish went to war with his brother the king of Sippar over one of them. The great queen of Ur, Nin-Nammu, had a necklace made of five, including those which had belonged to Gilgamesh; the goddess Semiramis was so affronted by the vanity of this that she struck Nin-Nammu dead and took them for herself. They caused so much dissension among the gods that in order to quiet the bickering, Ea ordered them scattered."

The Tavern Goddess paused, and fixed Ninshi with her eye. "I want these rubies. All of them. For each you bring me, I will tell you of the location of one of the herbs you desire."

Ninshi glared back. "I am no thief."

"No child, you are much worse than that. You are a murderer. And this will not be an easy task, but still I think you able. If I only needed some cutpurse, why I am worshipped by a great many of them. This will require cunning, and bloodshed, deceit and betrayal. Is there not a caravan song about you?

What will be destroyed belongs to the Servant
Who comes for the mother's fruit and takes it away.
She is a destroyer, a slayer of men.

I am not asking anything of you that is outside of your nature. A slayer slays. A betrayer betrays."

Ninshi sat very still, for many heartbeats. Miri was quiet, though the silence stretched painfully. Finally Ninshi nodded. "Yes, I will do this."

"Good. I thought you might. Let me make you a bundle of food, to eat on the road. You will be looking for the first stone in Emar, where it is owned by a merchant who is thought to be quite wealthy, even in that city of merchants. His name is Ota-Emari. How you obtain it or any of the Tears is unimportant. Steal it, buy it, cut his throat for it. When you have it, go to any tavern, and drop it into a cup of wine. It will come to me, and as you drink I will speak to you, telling you the location of one of your plants and the next ruby."

"Where is this Emar? Is it a city?" Miri scrambled to keep up with Ninshi, who strode through the early morning crowd of the city. Though it had seemed only an hour or two had passed talking to the Tavern Goddess, when they left it was sunrise.

"It is the next city on the river, on the banks where it widens. It is the sister to the city of Mari which is just a few days journey further downstream."

"There is truly a city with the same name as me?"

"It is close, though the word means a different thing in the language of your people. If I recall, your name means *treasured*, or maybe *gift*. In the language of the people who built the cities Mari means sunrise, and Emar means sunset." They walked past a fountain, surrounded by women who were filling narrow clay jugs from it and carrying them away on their heads. There was a great deal of jostling and much banter, most of it good-natured. For a moment Miri felt a stabbing pang of loss, remembering how her mother, her first mother, had gone to the well in the square each morning. Already the memory seemed faded and far away.

"Will we take a boat, then?"

"No, we will walk. I will try to find a caravan that we can travel with today. I do not like boats."

Past the well the street narrowed, and the buildings crowded in, taller and shuttered. Miri saw Ninshi put one hand on her purse and the other on her sword. Miri remembered to shift her pack to the front, and put one hand on it. The other she put on her knife. The crowd was thick, and twice Miri thought she saw furtive movement near a citizen's waist, what could be the sign of a cutpurse. They came out the other side unrobbed, into a market just waking up. Merchants and vendors were laying out their wares on tables and carpets; brightly painted jars and pots, knives and razors of bronze, swathes of colorful cloth, earrings and bangles inlaid with lapis and carnelian. Located on the westernmost crossing of the Euphrates, Caracamesh was a crossroads between the great cities of the Rivers to the east, the Khettites to the north, and the Twin Kingdoms of the Pharaohs to the south. Its market was spectacular.

Twice Ninshi had to take hold of Miri's arm and guide her away from some merchant's stall, the second time ungently. Once they were through the market they were at the gate, a different one than they had entered by the night before. They walked through the red-painted gateposts to the caravansary outside.

Ina
Part Two: Two Apes

Emar was dead.

They had been unable to find any caravan with which to travel, so Ninshi had purchased horses for them, and they had set off overland. The caravan masters had been of many accords: there was plague; no, there was a great army led by a demon; no, it was civil war. Whatever the truth, there was no one willing to go that way.

Miri had often seen horses, but when it came time to actually ride one she had frozen, terrified at the idea of trying to control all that power and beauty. Ninshi had been uncharacteristically patient with her, letting her make friends with the smaller of the two mares she purchased. The mare was patient, too, allowing Miri to woo her with small gifts of carrots and oats.

They traveled slowly the first two days, letting Miri gain confidence. By the end of the first she was sorer than she had ever in her life been, even the morning after Ninshi had first started training her with sword, knife, and spear. But that was nothing to the next morning, when Miri found she could not stand up from her bed, and quietly wept as she tried without success to rub out the pain in her thighs. She at last could stand, to find Ninshi watching her with amusement, and a glint of something else.

"We will take a rest from swordplay tonight, I think," said Ninshi. "I am feeling a little unused to riding."

Miri was grateful for the lie. So far as she could tell Ninshi never tired. On the day that they had met, her new mother had fought several men, and then walked with her, wounded, until they were safely out of the city. And it was Miri that night who had fallen asleep first, trying to keep eyes half open, fearing that if she slept she would awake once again a slave. She had prayed for Ninshi, having heard of her in a caravan song, and the next night Ninshi had indeed appeared in the caravansary by the Euphrates crossing where the slavers who owned Miri had rested. The morning after, she had summoned courage enough to bolt from the slavers when it looked like her prayed-for miracle was leaving, and then she had managed to gasp out a jumble of words that somehow had moved the figure of legend to offer a few coins for her.

The months had passed as they journeyed east in search of the plants that would perhaps free Ninshi from her bondage to the dreadful beast she served.

Few had even heard of the *shappatu*, the fabled herbs given to Noach so he might command the beasts after the deluge, and those few who had knew little other than their ancient names. Finally in desperation they had sought the help of the Protector of Carcamesh, whom Ninshi had known of from centuries past.

Who had sent them here, to this place of death.

Bones lay scattered by the roadside, bones of men and oxen and horses. Among them were broken carts and the charred and twisted remains of chariots. The road itself was torn, as if tilled by an insane farmer with a jagged plow. The turves and clumps of road surface dirt, packed hard by the centuries of trade and travel, were piled about, the tops of many scorched as if by fire. The city gates ahead lay in pieces, torn asunder and flung to the ground on each side.

"Look," said Ninshi. She fingered the broken-tooth talisman that hung about her neck. "The gates were burst from the inside."

Miri shifted on the riding blanket, hoping to ease her still-aching thighs. They hurt less now, but they had ridden since first light and it was past noon. "What does it mean?" she asked.

Ninshi was quiet for several breaths, then sighed. "I don't know," she said at last.

They rode slowly forward, toward the opening that gaped in the walls. As they drew closer Miri saw that the walls, which had seemed from a distance to be straight, actually slumped and bulged strangely as if something had caused them to melt. In places the mud bricks had tumbled from their courses to lie in heaps outside the wall.

They arrived at the gates. The horses, which had already started to fidget and dance, stopped dead. Miri could see that Ninshi's mare was particularly wide eyed, and seemed to be panting as if she had been recently run.

"We will tie the horses here."

Miri slid off her mare, relieved. Six days of practice had not been enough to make her a confident rider, and the mare's increased distress was frightening. She passed the lead rope through a piece of broken chariot wheel that lay trapped under a half-burnt pile of debris. Mari carefully looped the rope, tongue between her teeth as she concentrated on the knot Ninshi had taught her. "Easy for you to untie, hard for the horse," she had explained. It took a little longer because the rope kept snagging on a jagged piece of the wheel's bronze joining.

She looked up to find her mother standing perfectly still, staring through the gate. Her right hand held her drawn sword, her left grasped the talisman about her neck in a white-knuckled fist.

Miri hastily drew her knife and held it as she had practiced, close to her body, tip down. With her left hand she gathered her shift, drawing it so that it bunched up under her belt on her left hip, but was tight against her right, so that her knife might not be caught in its folds.

"Come," Ninshi said, and strode forward.

Inside was as chaotic as out. Buildings were burnt, or tumbled down. Few seemed to be more than half intact. Bones, broken furniture and other debris choked doorways. They made their way to the ziggurat, visible over the ruined rooftops on a hillock at the center of the city. As they drew closer Miri could see that its top was scorched and broken. A dark stain ran down its stairs from the top nearly all the way to the ground.

Twice they were forced to find a way around the piles of brick and debris that choked the street.On the second detour they found a small market, largely intact, with bangles and rugs and clay jars still laid out as if for sale. In the center was a large table. The wooden, clay, and ivory household idols it once held were swept to the side, resting in a broken heap on the ground. They had been replaced on the table by six human arms, with their right hands still attached. On the forefinger of each hand was a ring, the stone prised out. They were arranged in merchant fashion in imitation of the market goods around them, as if to attract some casual buyer of severed limbs. The sun had desiccated them, and the leathery flesh was split, revealing the bones beneath.

They made their way back to the street to the ziggurat. Where not choked with rubble it was wide. The trees which lined it were all dead; some withered as if by drought and others shattered and scorched by lightning.

"We are for the far side of the temple. Matar Kubileya said that the house of Ota-Emari will be south of the ziggurat, marked by two apes." It was the first either of them had spoken since entering the city. Though she spoke softly, Ninshi's voice echoed harshly. Her eyes widened. "No birds," she whispered.

Mari listened carefully. Indeed, other than the soft sighing of the wind there was no sound at all.

A few hundred steps from the ziggurat mound the street ended abruptly at the edge of a deep depression. It was perfectly circular, and at least a hundred steps across, perhaps half that much in depth. The inside of the pit was black and shone in the midday sun. Ninshi knelt, and with the hilt of her sword rapped on the side. The surface cracked around her blow in a star pattern, white at the center. "Glass," she whispered.

They made their way carefully around the crater. Occasionally they found smaller, outlying craters, perhaps the width of a large man's outstretched arms. On the far side the street resumed, then split three ways, one up the hill to the temple, one each side around. A stain of black flowed down this side of the ziggurat as well. As they stumbled and climbed over the wreckage that filled the side street, the wind shifted, and the heavy stench of long-clotted blood filled Miri's nostrils. They hurried past broken buildings and a square where the well at the center was heaped over with blackened bones.

On the far side Ninshi stopped. If anything the destruction was even more complete on this side. Miri tugged at her sleeve and pointed. To one side were the remains of a large house, walled, with pillars at the gateposts. On one stood a large statue of an ape. The other pillar was broken, but at its base was a matching statue, broken jaggedly across the middle, with its head defaced and its limbs knocked off.

They passed between the pillars, to find themselves in a courtyard. At its center stood a fountain, dead now and only half-filled with stinking green water. The whole front of the house had fallen down, or been pulled down, revealing the rooms inside. They gingerly picked through the wreckage, going from room to room, but the only thing remarkable was the absence of human remains. There was broken furniture and pottery, and it looked like someone had built a campfire recently in the center of the largest room, ignoring the fireplace that stood at one side. Ota-Emari, if this was indeed his house, was either dead or had fled.

"We will look to see if there are any other houses nearby marked with apes, but I doubt we will find any. This is far from the land of the Nubians, where such beasts dwell, and it is not a totem I would expect to find common." Even inside the house, Ninshi whispered. Miri did not need to ask her why.

As they passed back to the house gates, something about the broken pillar caught Miri's eye. She bent down, and found herself looking at a gap where the pillar had been knocked out of position. Underneath the square base was a cavity, and something gleamed inside. With the pillar askew, she could see that one of the bricks that paved the courtyard was loose. Gently she pulled it up, and found herself looking at a perfectly square hidey-hole, perhaps a hand span across. Inside were a small leather bag and a scroll, held with a yellow metal clasp. She pulled them from their resting place, and looked up to find her mother watching. She started to speak but thought better. If Ninshi could only bring herself to whisper in this place, then she would not speak at all.

Ninshi made a head motion toward the bag, and Miri opened its strings and spilled its contents into her palm. Inside were several metal slugs, mostly copper, but a few of silver and two of gold.

The scroll Ninshi took, and examined. The clasp seemed to be of gold and was well-made. It opened easily, and she unrolled it to peer at the writing inside. "No map," she whispered, and rolled it back up. "We will have to find a priest or a merchant to read it."

Miri nodded. While it had never occurred to her that there might be anything that Ninshi couldn't do, few outside the walls of the temples who weren't involved in civil business could read. Even in the Two Kingdoms where she had been born, where the Pharaohs seemed to write on every available flat surface, usually it was only the scribes and a few merchants who could read what they said.

They walked into the street. Ninshi stopped abruptly. In a semicircle around the gateway, standing each an arms-width apart were a dozen men. They were dressed in white kilts, soiled by travel, and sleeveless wool tunics with brass discs sewn to them. Each wore a leather helmet, the once-bright paint on them faded and stained. They all were armed with spears, which were held ready, and Miri could see bright bronze daggers at their belts. Their shields were round, with brass or bronze bosses at the centers, painted in the same formerly bright colors as their helms. Their beards were plaited and oiled, cut square at the ends in the fashion of the men of Ugarit, though they were darker and of rounder face that the people of that city.

"Hakash!" hissed the one in the center. *"Umrii itsach ha-diran?"*

Ninshi shook her head. *"Onephi, ha-Babylosh.* And this child does not speak Khettish. But I do speak the language of the Ibaru, as does the child."

"We are not Ibaru. They departed our land several lifetimes ago. And I doubt that you are Babylonian. But the tongue of the Ibaru will do. It is close enough to what we speak at home that all will understand. What is your business here?"

"I might ask the same of you, but the answer is clear to both of us. We are travelers who have come upon this place and we seek to understand what has happened."

The leader frowned and nodded. "I do not like speaking here. It is as if our words are snatched from our lips and drowned in Hell. Come with us. You will speak with our prince."

Ninshi nodded in return, and sheathed her sword. The shoulders of the leader dropped noticeably, and his men lowered the points of their spears from ready. They formed up in two lines, with Miri and Ninshi at the center, and trotted off in the direction opposite from which the two of them had entered the city.

The desolation was greater, but the distance to the gate at that end of the city was far less. Soon they were at the river gate, and then outside the walls. These gates, too, had been cast down and burst apart, seemingly from the inside.

Here, the river was restrained by a breakwater, much as would be found at an ocean port. At the docks the masts of sunken river-going boats jutted at strange angles from the water. Some had tatters of sail attached, as if they had been sunk while attempting to get under way. The great warehouses were all burned to the ground, their goods looted or destroyed.

Here too the road was plowed up and lined with the bones of men, horses, oxen, wagons and chariots. The captain led them up the rise from the river, where perhaps a thousand steps away they could see a small circle of pavilions set in camp on a hill above the city. Thin lines of smoke rose above the camp into the sky, and as they drew nearer they could see that it was ringed by spears set into the ground, hung with horsetail banners and ribbons of brightly colored cloth.

The captain marched the soldiers through the camp to the large multi-colored pavilion that rested at its center. “Wait,” he commanded, and speaking a word to one of the two large guards who stood at each side of its door, passed inside. Beside the pavilion was a large gilt chariot, with a canopy rigged above, its tongue resting on a large rock.

Though busy, the camp around them was unusually quiet. Several hands-full of men came and went, all of them armed like their escorts and all of them worried looking. Across the camp's center, Miri could see a large open-air kitchen. At its center a calf roasted over a low fire, and to one side in the embers sat a large clay pot, sides blackened, with steam rising from its open top. Her stomach growled, and she realized that they had not eaten since sunrise. The dead city had banished all thoughts of hunger until now.

The return of the captain broke her daydreams of meat and bread.

“You will come with me.” He motioned to them to follow and stepped back into the tent.

Inside it was dark and noticeably cooler. Miri blinked rapidly and things came into focus. The tent was floored with heavy carpets, and curtained off into sections with elaborately sewn cloth. A robed man stood at a table in center of the open space. He was short and stocky, bareheaded except for the strip of red cloth that tied back his hair. His beard was thick, black where it wasn't grey.

"It has been a great many years, *Muttaliku.*" His voice was low and soft, but carried.

"Indeed it has, Great Priest." Then, to Miri's utter astonishment, Ninshi knelt.

Miri gawped open-mouthed until her mother's hard hand slapped her on the back, then knelt in imitation. She was sure that the red glow of her face was lighting up the tent. She didn't want to look up, but her curiosity overcame her humiliation.

"Rise. What brings you to this place, and what can you tell me of its destruction?"

Ninshi got to her feet. "I fear I know nothing more than what you already must. It looks as though it was struck by earthquake, civil war, invasion, and drought. I saw holes in the earth, as if a great fire fell from the sky, and trees blasted by lightning."

The priest peered at her sharply. "This is not the doing of the beast you serve?"

Ninshi shook her head. "No, great Malki-tzédek. This is beyond his power, I think. We found it this way."

He nodded. "You will take meat with me, and rest. I will need to know the story of how you came here, and I will tell you what I know. Together we may learn something."

The next few hours passed quickly. Food was brought to them as they sat with Malki-tzédek on cushions. Miri lost track of Ninshi's story as she ate greedily. The meat was seasoned with unfamiliar spices, at once sweet and hot, served with balls of sweet rice wrapped in boiled mustard leaves. At some point the priest sent men for their horses.

"...and so when we came to the house we found nothing," finished Ninshi. "But as we left, the child here spied a hidey-hole. In it we found a handful of trading metal and this scroll." She handed it to Malki-tzédek.

He removed the clasp, holding it up to the light which streamed into the tent from a smoke-hole above. "No more than a clasp," he said, and set it aside. He opened the scroll, peered at it. "I can read this," he said, and bent his head, tracing lines of writing with his finger.

"It is written in the language of Akkad, not surprising as that is what is spoken, or rather was spoken here. It is a missive to someone named Ishkabal, whom I take from the text is a caravan master for the merchant Ota-Emari. After some hasty greetings, it says:

> *The city has gone mad. After the earthquake, the priests of the sky gods and their followers turned on the city elders, and the streets are filled with rioters, mad with disease and insane with thirst, as the wells have all failed. The storms are unrelenting; never before have I seen lightning without cloud or rain. Mercifully our house alone has been spared. Neither rioter nor lightning has entered our walls, and the fountain in the courtyard still yields sweet water. This dawn found both city gates besieged by a vast host, armed with spear and sling, and many horses and chariots. They chant the name of Namtar, servant of Ereshkigal, and from within our walls a great many have taken to chanting with them.*
>
> *We are fleeing. We will leave by the way prepared. If you find this, join us at the second oasis, past the place of the ancients. We will wait there for you until the change of the next moon. Your sister is safe with us, as is your mother.*

"It is signed with a seal-stamp of the figure of an ape."

Ninshi nodded thoughtfully. "So we learn much, though not enough. Whoever has heard of so many cataclysms befalling a city at once? I thought Namtar just a name in old stories, as he may be, but who in this day regards him? Is he, or someone acting in his name responsible for more than conquest of this city? I have seen the God whom you serve rain fire on a city, and utterly destroy it, but this has such an odor of wickedness that I cannot believe He is responsible."

"You are correct. This is chaotic and brutal. What else can we surmise from this missive?"

"Our merchant does not much trust his servant. He offers both bribe and threat to ensure his obedience, the metal as bribe, the threat of his family as hostage. He must have much in the way of goods. A good caravan can make even a wealthy man wealthier, and to one starting over it could be even more important."

"There is another thing," Malki-tzédek said. He called for more wine, then continued. "This 'prepared way'. When we arrived here, I sent several of my men around the city walls before we entered. On the east side, one of them found a broken shack leaning against the wall, not unusual, but with the tracks of men and camels leading from it. That a hovel barely an arm's span across could hold even one animal, let alone the number of camels, horses, sheep and men that from the tracks there issued from it was curious indeed, so he investigated. Inside he found a stone-lined tunnel that led under the wall. He followed it back until the light from the entrance failed him, but by shouting determined that it went much farther on."

"Did he mark where the tracks led?"

"Yes. In the morning we will take you there. They lead east, across the desert. A merchant might have a secret way for goods of uncertain provenance, perhaps, or just as an advantage over competitors. The mention of a second oasis would seem to confirm this."

"Very well. How then, my lord, did you come to be here, so far north from your land?"

Malki-tzédek shifted on his pillow. "We had heard reports from travelers of cities that were no longer living. This is the third such we have found; two other cities, both ports on the middle sea, have been destroyed."

"In this fashion?"

"Not so completely as Emar, but yes. Both of them were smaller. From the second we followed the tracks of the besieging host as they made their way here. Though in both other cases they seem to have attacked from the sea, here they made a line, straight as an arrow's flight, overland from the walls of one city to another.

"I have never seen savagery like this. The host destroyed everything in its path, farm, field and waterway. That calf we ate today was one of the few cattle we gleaned in following, left by omission along the way.

"From travelers' stories and runners sent to kingdoms north, we have learned that this scourge, and whatever guides it, has been ravaging the north for several dozens of years. Cities, which are less frequent there and often made of wood, have been burned, tribes displaced, and trade disrupted. Of late there has been little of the tin needed for making bronze, which comes mostly from mines in northern lands. When there is no bronze for weapons, how will we defend against this host?"

"What will you do?" asked Ninshi.

"We will return to our land in the south, and prepare as best we can. It may be many more lifetimes before it makes its way to us. Or it may never come so far south. The path of its departure from here leads north, back into the wastelands. We will have to trust in God, as should you."

Ninshi looked down. "I cannot."

"Cannot, or will not? Can you look into your heart and not see truth?"

"I see truth, priest. You cannot know what I see. My heart tells me that when I am in your presence I cannot feel the pull of the talisman, that it becomes nothing more than the tooth of an ancient beast, just as it was when I traveled with the Well Digger, when he tithed to you, the righteous priest, lifetimes ago. I rested then at night, unhaunted by the faces of those I have slain.

"You cannot know. For lifetime after lifetime I have slept only when I could no longer stay awake. Awake I cannot recall their names. Asleep I cannot forget them. But I know that tonight, for the first time in the two or more hundreds of years since we last met, I will sleep, unhaunted. And I know that if I would but give in, submit to your God, I could sleep every night as if I were once again as innocent as this child beside me.

"But I cannot! Would your God give me back my love, the boy whom the Beast has held these lifetimes of men? Would he give me revenge against the Fallen whose beastly form I serve? Can you guarantee this, priest? Say you can, and I will follow, but if you cannot, then your God is of no use to me, believe in him however much I do. He can give me peace, yes, and of all the gods I have ever heard of or seen that is more than they ever could do, and so I believe. But I need more than peace."

Malki-tzédek shook his head. "Peace is what He offers, and hope. But I do not know what would happen other than that. It may be that all you have lost will be restored. It may be in His wisdom he sees another path for you. I do not know. But you do. You know the truth, *Muttaliku.* It is up to you to seek it, or turn away."

Ninshi was quiet for long moments. Her chest rose and fell slowly, and other than a few sounds from the camp outside, there was silence. She sighed.

"Malki-tzédek, my old friend. You speak the truth, as always. I thank you for your wisdom, for the meat you have shared, and yes, for the grateful night I will sleep as your guest. But my steps are already on the path they will take. If I can, I will destroy the beast and free my love. If I cannot, then I will die seeking it. In the morning we will take your leave, and pursue the merchant Ota-Emari."

The priest nodded. "I weep for you."

"There is no need. I weep for myself."

Ala
Part Three: "*Who comes for the mother's fruit*"

"Yes, I know that you have questions, but I am not yet awake. Can you not wait until we have ridden for a while to ask them?" Ninshi twisted and stretched, her face still puffy and eyes bleary. Her horse gleamed beneath her, combed and washed by Malki-tzédek's servants during the night. Her glance caught Miri's and she laughed, the first time in the months they had been together that she had done more than smile grimly.

"Pity," she smiled. "I shall take pity on you, as you have managed to hold in your curiosity for so very long." Ninshi's smile was startling. Her teeth were whole, and perfectly white against her sun-weathered face, and the wrinkles of her smile hid the worst of her scars. "Ask."

"Who is he, this priest?"

Ninshi looked down, to make certain of their path. It was hardly needed, though, as the trail was straight and easily followed. It ran east, and slightly north, into the heart of the desert that separated this stretch between the Tigris and the Euphrates. Farther south and east the land between the rivers was lush and fertile, but here it was rocky, barren and untraveled.

"I am surprised you do not know of him. He is the priest to whom the father of your people gave a tenth."

Miri frowned. "The father of my people?"

"Yes, *Tudhulu* he was called when I traveled with him, *Father of Nations*. Though the name seemed mocking at the time, as his wife, though comely, was barren and not quiet about it."

"Is this priest like you, then, unaging?"

"He is unaging, yes, but not at all like me. He is without father, without mother, without descent, having neither beginning of days, nor end of life. He has said that someday there will come another, but until then he rules as priest and prince in a city near the land of the Pharoahs. Like him I live long, yes, but it is under a curse."

"The name he called you, *Muttaliku.* Is that your name, the one you have forgotten?"

Ninshi's face stiffened. "No child, it is not. My name is what you have given me, Nin-Sinnus. The name I was given as a child is lost. *Muttaliku* is an ancient word, a desert word. It means *traveler,* or perhaps *wanderer.* It is used to describe those who are lost or who journey aimlessly through the waste, without home or family."

Miri nodded. "I like the name I gave you better, too."

They rode in the trail of the merchant for two days, finding in the evening of the third an oasis, just as the scroll had indicated. Though small, with brackish water and only a few grey shrubs for shelter, it was welcome after the unrelenting dusty brown of the wasteland. The low tough grass was sparse, but it was enough for grazing the two horses.

"Five days, maybe six since they were here," Ninshi said. "If we are quick, we will easily catch them at the next oasis before the changing of the moon."

They rested there, refilled their water skins with the harsh-tasting water of the small spring, and left before dawn.

Long before the sun had reached the center of the sky, they could see ahead the beginning of a series of low, flat hills, brown and irregular. As they rode closer, Miri could see that part of the irregularity came from many large stones that thrust up from the hilltops, almost square, almost smooth, but tumbled and broken. The trail they followed led right between them.

"We will stop here," Ninshi said. "Eat, drink, and empty your bladder and bowels, if you can. The place ahead is not the place for any of those things. We must waste no time. We need to be through these hills before nightfall."

"What is this place? Are there bandits?" Miri slid off her horse and reached for the water skin that hung over the mare's haunches.

Ninshi drank, rinsed her mouth and spat. "This is a place even the bravest bandit could not abide," she said. "When I was a child, this was the place that mothers used to threaten wayward children. I do not know the truth of it, but I have been told by those even older than I that this was one of the places of wickedness that caused Enlil to send the Deluge. It is what remains of a city, perhaps even larger than Great Ur, but whatever the cause of its destruction, flood, war or earthquake, I know this: evil lives there now. I have passed this way before, and always I have dreaded it."

It was another dead place. This time, however, Miri was really frightened. There were no bones to bear witness, no lightning-blasted trees, just mute stones and silence. The longer they rode, the heavier the sense of dread became. Sometimes she imagined something flitting just out of sight, glimpsed at the corner of her eye, but always she knew that whatever lurked in these low hills was still, silent and filled with anger and hatred. Hatred at her very existence, anger that she still walked and ate and breathed.

Hours passed, and the sun grew lower. They passed hill after hill, each the same brown, lumpy form pierced by great angry stones. Some seemed to be almost faces, screaming in silence, others vaguely resembled beasts, in forms half-imagined and never seen by daylight or sanity.

Miri had to pee, badly. "Just one more hill," she told herself. Then when that was past and they were still among them, "Just one more." Even the horses seemed to know, and held their water. Finally, as the sun was more than half over the horizon and the shadows of the great stones had begun to reach toward them with fingers of darkness and dread, they were through. Miri squirmed in her saddle, determined to say nothing but increasingly unable to stay still.

The sun was nearly gone and the final glimmers of daylight flickered among the shadows when Ninshi stopped her horse. The last hill rose a thousand or more paces behind, invisible in the dark but still felt at their backs.

"Far enough, I think," Ninshi said. "I hate that place."

Miri was too busy scrambling off her horse and running behind the nearest rock to listen. When she emerged, sighing and relieved, she found that Ninshi was already building a fire. In a short time the last of the calf's meat given to them by Malki-tzédek warmed on a rock near its center, and a few wilted onions rested at its side.

Miri felt empty and tired, but she found herself unable to do more than nibble. Something about the night made her fear sleep, as if by laying her head down she would somehow be surrendering to something incredibly old and dreadful.

"Hobble the horses, then sleep, child. We are safe here. We did nothing to invite the dwellers in that place of evil. They may call, but they cannot follow."

In spite of her mother's words, Miri slept fitfully. Several times she awoke to see the fire burnt low and Ninshi regarding her, sword across her lap. She was used to this; Ninshi truly slept little. It did nothing to quell her fears. Finally she fell into a dream-filled sleep, disturbed by images that repeated over and over, not terrifying in themselves but ugly and inescapable.

She awakened cold in the pre-dawn stillness. Ninshi lay bundled in an old blanket by the fire, which guttered and flickered, giving nearly no light. The sky was streaked above, ready for the new day. She was not rested, but the growing light brought a lightening of her spirit, and by the time Ninshi arose, dark circles under her eyes, Miri had regained at least a portion of her normal cheerfulness.

They fed the horses and themselves, and rode on. By mid-day, Ninshi was frowning, stopping every few hundred steps to examine the ground. Finally she motioned Miri from her horse, and pointed out small marks in the dust. "These are new," she said. "They are unlike anything I have seen before. Look at the narrow marks these tracks leave." Miri nodded, though in truth she could determine only that the tracks were there, and seemed a different shape than the camel prints, hoof scrapes and sandal marks that Ninshi had pointed out before.

"They are followed. We must hurry. It is important that we get to the merchants before whatever stalks them does. I do not know what it is that follows them, but if it came from the Hills of Stones, it cannot be good."

The horses were already tired, and could not be pushed much more, but still they tried. Ninshi gave them extra water, and the last of the oats they had purchased in Carcamesh, but the heat and barren earth, without greenery for them to graze, and the harsh pace took a visible toll. The horses panted, and stank with sweat. Finally Ninshi's mare took a limp. She dismounted, and had Miri do the same, and they led them over the broken plain.

As darkness settled on the second night after leaving the ancient city, Miri spotted a glow on the horizon ahead. The horses were nearly dead, and Miri didn't feel far behind. Her feet hurt, and she was very thirsty. Ninshi had decided at that dawn to only allow them to wet their mouths every hand of the sun, hoping to eke what they could from the half-skin of water that remained to them.

Miri pointed at the light, and Ninshi nodded. "Drink now, all you like. Whatever is left, divide between the horses. Yonder is our oasis. We will rest here for a while, then make our way there. I fear there is little time; the trackers have grown too close to their prey."

They led the horses through the dark, aided by the nearly full moon. The light cast by it flooded the plain, making shadow mountains fall from knee-high rocks. As they drew closer they could see that the light was reflected off cliffs beyond. The oasis rested in a depression where the slope of the plain descended to an ancient river bed that had long ago ran along the cliffs.

Ninshi held out her hand, and Miri stopped. "Hobble the horses," she whispered. Miri struggled in the dark with the ropes. The horses no longer cared, but she was tired, and it was very hard to see. Finally Ninshi noticed her difficulty and held the far legs of each mare as Miri looped the hobbles around them.

"String your bow. Bring nothing else, save your knife." Ninshi strung hers as well, and they made their way into the darkness toward the light of the camp at the base of the cliff.

Miri moved slowly through the darkness. She wished that she could move as smoothly as Ninshi, who seemed to glide between the rocks. Her feet hurt, which took away any feeling of grace, and the five arrows she had thrust under her belt beneath her right arm kept poking her. Still, she somehow managed to keep up and soon they were among the scraggly trees that lined the verge of the cut below.

She felt her mother's hand against her chest and she stopped. Beneath them lay a circle of tents around a spring, trees sprouting randomly around them. In the center a fire burned, larger and higher than normal this late, when the camp seemed to be asleep. Sheep, a few horses, and camels were staked to a picket beyond. Near the fire a guard nodded, seated on a downed tree that seemed to be the source of fuel for the fire. Other than that, the camp showed no life.

"Find me the guards," whispered Ninshi. "There are four. No, five."

Miri closed her eyes and thought. Ninshi had taught her that the best way to defeat an enemy was to see what he saw. The camp was simple. No approach from the cliff side, not at night. The horses would act as guards themselves, so a guard there was not needed.

"There," she pointed, opening her eyes. "By the big rock, and two more at the trees, there and there. Number four rests just below us; I can see the top of his head over that little rise. Five is a cheat. He lies nodding right there, on the log."

"Good. There is something else, something important about the guard just below us."

Miri peered through the darkness. The man's shape was only partially visible. His head was wholly clear, but he rested lazily against the knob of earth. Was he asleep? He was so still. Too still.

"He is dead!" Miri hissed, surprised.

Ninshi pointed, then nocked an arrow to her bowstring. "There. There is what killed him, I think."

At first Miri saw nothing, then a dark figure flitted between two trees, halfway down the slope. In the fleeting moment she glimpsed it, she could not make out whether it was man or woman, or even if it was human.

"That is what followed them. We may be too late."

She stood up, drew, and released the arrow. "Awake, the camp!" she shouted, and nocked another arrow. "Awake, awake!" She shouted, and shot again at the figure, which had stopped in confusion near the largest tent. She missed again, but as the arrow clattered past the creature looked up at the direction the arrow had come. Miri did not doubt that the pale blue eyes that pierced the darkness saw them.

Answering shouts rose from the camp. Men staggered from the outer tents to rally at the center, and the nodding guards jolted up from their slumber.

The figure was caught between them, taller than any of them, but dark, withered and thin. It charged at the guard who had slept on the log, but he drove it back with his spear. Another guard slashed at it with his sword, and when the others saw that he did not melt away they too rushed in, blades rising and falling.

It did not die easily. Men were flung from it, and more than once it broke free, only to be dragged back down into the swarm of guards. It at last was still and the guards stepped away, panting, to stare at the figure at their feet.

"The camp!" Ninshi shouted, and they made their way down the bank and into the light. Men peered at them with wide eyes. Miri could see why they were afraid. Whatever it was that they had killed was terrifying in form. It was longer and thinner than a man. Its naked form was hacked and torn, but even so it was clear that this was a thing unnatural. Its leathery skin was grey in the firelight, and covered with tumors and boils. The legs and arms were too long, and both the feet and the hands of the creature ended in tapering claws. Its head was turned up, and its wide mouth was open, revealing too many teeth, sharp and needle-like, in sets of rows. It had no nose, only open nostrils, and its eyes were huge.

"What is it?" whispered someone.

Ninshi spat. "It is an *Ekimmu*, a ghul from ancient days. It has been following you since the Hills of Stones. We were lost and crossed your trail, sought to follow you. We picked up sign of this one two days ago."

"What did it want?" asked another.

"It was here for murder. It would have killed you all in your sleep, as it did your guard, up there."

They stared at her for a moment, then one of them started shouting orders. More wood was thrown on the fire, men were sent to bring the body of the slain guard down, and new guards were posted.

"You will be my guest. I am called Ota, of the city of Emar."

"I am Ninshi, and this is Miri."

The men brought the body of the slain guard into the light. His body was withered, as if he had been dead for days rather than minutes, and his throat was torn out.

"You must cut off his head, and the head of the creature which killed him," Ninshi said, "Else neither will stay dead. Burn them both, but if you valued this man in life, burn them separately."

Ota gave quick orders. In moments there were two new fires, at the downwind end of the camp. He turned to the nearest of his followers. "Bring salt and bread. We must honor these who have saved us all." He was tall, handsome in an angular fashion, with a neatly trimmed short beard and hair oiled and braided. He was dressed in a cotton sleeping shirt.

Miri caught a glimpse of motion at the opening of the largest tent. From behind the flap a girl peered, about her age, eyes wide. Miri smiled, and the girl's mouth formed into a perfect circle, and she darted back inside. Miri looked down at herself. Her shift was filthy and travel-stained. She had ripped the hem on a sharp stone a few days before, and had sewn it back poorly. On the right side her shift was pulled down, snagged by the bronze head of one of the arrows thrust into her belt. Her legs were bare and filthy. She looked at her hands. They were newly callused, from rein and sword and bow. Her fingernails were black rimmed and broken. A stray strand of hair drifted into her face, and she licked her palm and smoothed it back into place.

"I must look like some wild thing that has wandered in from the desert!" she thought. She looked at her mother. Though dirty and stained, she still was neat, her hair braided and oiled and her face and hands clean. "I will do better," she thought.

"Sit, my friends, here in the place of honor. Soon it will be light, and we will break our fast. We have slaughtered a lamb, and we have dates and milk. How did you come here? Not afoot, surely."

"Our horses are hobbled, just over the rise, there. I feared they would call to their kind, as horses do, and so warn the creature who followed you."

"I will have them fetched, and fed."

At sunrise, Ota had ablution bowls brought to them. Miri washed her face and hands, and was appalled to see the water turn from clear to murky grey. She must be filthy! Worse yet, she caught her reflection in the water. Her hair was untrimmed and knotted in clumps, and her nose, forehead and cheeks were sun burnt and peeling.

The mood of the camp was cheerful, as only people who have narrowly escaped some dreadful thing can be. They gathered, guards, merchant and women in the center of camp on carpets laid out around a tree. Ninshi and Miri were seated in places of honor, nearest the food, and they ate.

Miri loved dates, and these were big and sweet. In front of each of them had been set a bowl of milk, and she paused often to wash down mouthfuls of the tangy fruit. Finally she was full, and happier than she had been for days.

Around them the merchant camp laughed and smiled as they ate. Ninshi sat upright, as always, and ate quietly. If their hosts noticed that they were less than talkative, they gave no indication. Finally, Ota clapped his hands, and called for silence.

"We owe these two much," he said. "And they must be rewarded. I then so swear, that whatever I have that they desire shall be theirs. Ask of me any one thing, and as Enki Himself is my witness, so it shall be yours."

Around them Ota's people nodded and smiled. This was the sort of oath given by rich men and kings, and Miri could see that it pleased them. Even the hard-bitten caravan guards, returned from their terror last night to their more normal and usual air of competent boredom seemed impressed.

"Let us start with the child, here. Tell me little one, what gift can I give you? What is your desire?"

"Anything?" asked Miri.

"Anything," smiled Ota.

"A comb!" blurted Miri, then face burning, she looked down, humiliated.

All around them the people laughed. Ota clapped his hands in delight. "A comb, you say? Treasure indeed! You shall have it, and more. My daughter seems to be of a size with you. Let us have you bathed, and new clothes brought you, a shift for travel and a dress for beauty. My wives shall dress your hair and give you oils to take with you so that your skin may be softened. And of course, you shall have a comb!"

She was led off, confused and embarrassed, to the largest tent. "When that is done, we shall see what it is that your mother desires." Ota announced to applause. "In the meantime, rest here as we feast."

An hour passed, in delightful activity, as Ota's wives and servants fussed around her. She had bathed before, of course, but had not been bathed by others since earliest childhood. Her hair was washed, oiled and combed out, ends trimmed and evened. Scented oils were rubbed into her skin, and the nails on her fingers and toes were trimmed and covered with an oil that hardened into a pearly gloss.

As she was being fitted for her new shift, which indeed needed only a little taking in to fit, the girl who had peered from behind the flap earlier came shyly up, and thrust something into her hand. Miri looked down. In her hand rested a small comb, made of dark, oiled wood. She looked up, to thank her, but she was gone.

Miri returned to the feast, head held high. On her feet were new sandals. Her hair was held back by a red band of cloth that matched the trim on her new traveling shift. Under her arms she carried a folded dress of light green cotton, trimmed with tufts of wool and small shells. Her belt was newly blacked and polished, and though they had tried to get her to surrender her knife, they had failed. It was thrust into her belt, but polished and clean the bronze of its blade shone brightly in the mid-morning sun.

As she walked back into the circle, the people smiled at her, and nodded in approval. Ota laughed when he saw her, and smiled brightly through his beard. "A transformation indeed!" He turned to Ninshi. "What then shall we give to you?"

"Bring us our horses, for we have urgent business that needs our attention and we must be on our way. Before we leave, I will tell you what it is that I desire."

Ota's face fell, but then he smiled. "Of course," he said. "Business is business, and must be attended to. Fetch their horses, and make sure that they have food and full water bags."

The horses, while still thin and tired looking, were brushed and clean, and fresh water and green grass had done much to revive them. Ninshi motioned for Miri to get on her horse, and she looked down at her and Ota as they talked.

"What then may I give you," he asked. Around and behind him the smiling people of the camp looked on.

"Anything, you said." Ninshi had one hand on her horse's neck.

"As I have sworn, before Enki and my people."

"I desire a ruby. It is about the size of the end of my finger, tear shaped and reddest red."

Ota's smile froze on his face, and the people were instantly silent. Several of the guards stepped forward, but Ota waved them back. "How do you know of this?" he spat. "What betrayal is this?"

"You said anything."

"I did, but you should think hard before asking this of me. This treasure is not for gifting."

Ninshi's hand went to her sword. "Is your word then, and your oath worth nothing?"

Ota's face went very dark, and around him the people muttered in anger. "Bring from my couch the small casket which lies beneath," he gritted to the nearest guard.

"This is not wisdom, you asking this. I do not know how you know of this ruby, or of my owning it, but I do not look kindly toward betrayal or treachery. I have sworn an oath, and I shall honor it, but take care that you never cross my path again."

The guard returned from the tent with a small box. From it Ota drew a small silver chain with a metal cage pendant. Inside the cage flashed a ruby, hearts-blood red. He flung it at Ninshi, chain and all, and she caught it and tucked it into the pouch at her belt.

She swung up on her horse, and they rode out of the camp in hostile silence.

They rode south, along the dry river bed. After a short while, the cliffs on their left ended, and they found themselves back on the plain, the only sign of the ancient river a slight depression meandering south towards the Tigris.

"Listen carefully child. We must look for a place that is easily defended. We have only a few hours before Ota's regret overcomes his pride, and he sends men after us to fetch back his ruby. I am guessing that they will not approach us until sunset. Ota offered us guesting before dawn, so he will be able to argue to himself that his protection ends with the sun of this day. He will not come himself, but he will send someone trusted, most likely the captain of his guard. That way, if murder is involved, he can claim to himself at least that it was accidental."

"Will he do that? Have us killed? I liked him."

"Here is a lesson for you. Like or dislike does not matter. Men kill other men, and sometimes they will try to kill you. We have taken a great prize from him, and in the end he is a merchant after all, no more honest than he must be."

It was nearly dark before they found a place that satisfied Ninshi. Against the river bank stood three man-high rocks, washed there in ancient deluge. Two of them were pushed together, and the third stood in front, making approach difficult for more than one person at a time.

For some time they had been able to see dust rising behind them. "One hour, no more," announced Ninshi. "They will be here just at sunset."

They tethered the horses behind the rocks. "Bow, I think for you, but have your knife ready. They may pretend to come in friendship at first.

"But Ninshi, I am terrible with the bow."

"Yes, but they will not know this, and it may keep them from approaching from the sides. Even if you never hit any of them, arrows flying at them are usually sufficient to make men cautious."

"Should we have a fire?" Miri asked. "Will we be able to see to fight?"

"A fire would only blind us, and make us better targets. We need them to come close, and if there are not too many, I should be able to kill enough of them to discourage Ota from sending any more."

Miri could see, past the rock, figures of men on horseback riding closer in the gathering darkness. They stopped a hundred paces away, and several dismounted, leaving two to hold their horses.

"A final thing," whispered Ninshi. "If I fall, let them take you. Your fate will be no worse than it would have been before you met me."

"I will not!" Miri hissed. "You will not fall, but if you did, I would stand over you until you could rise again, even if it meant being stabbed a thousand times." Miri was surprised at the ferocity in her own voice. Apparently so was Ninshi, who glanced down at her for a moment. It was difficult to read her expression at the best of times, and in the shadows of the failing day it was impossible.

"Very well, then, my little bow maiden. Do not let any of them get close enough to seize you, but if they do try to keep a hand free. A man will count on his strength and your small size. Let him. I have shown you how you may overcome this. Your knife must be thrust hard up along his leg, where it joins his body, and twisted if you can. A man wounded that way will seldom fight anymore, and he will be dead in twenty heartbeats."

Miri shook her head in agreement. Her heart was pounding, and after a moment she remembered to slow and deepen her breathing as Ninshi had taught her. She stood slightly behind and to the left of her, bow in hand with six arrows thrust into the sand in front of her and a seventh at the ready.

"Traveler!" called a deep voice from the group of men ahead. They moved slowly forward, resolving themselves into five of the caravan guards from Ota's camp. Four carried spears and small round shields. Their captain carried the same triangular sword he had used to hack at the creature the night before.

Ninshi said nothing, her breathing deep and slow. The men drew closer. Miri recognized several of them. They were unsmiling and grim.

"Traveler, we have come for the ruby. I offer you gold and silver in exchange. Give us what we ask, and you shall continue unharmed. We wish you no ill."

"Neither do I wish ill of you," replied Ninshi. "So if you go now, and return to your camp, I will not kill you."

The men all laughed, a harsh, nasty sound. Miri knew that laugh, though she had never heard it before. It was the music of murder.

The guard captain stepped forward, two of the spearman behind him. The other two circled to each side, trying to find a clear path past the rocks.

"Shoot them," Ninshi said, and Miri pulled back and let fly her arrow. She did not wait to see where it went, but as she reached for the next one heard it clatter on the rocks beyond the guards. She looked up, drew and released, the bow string slapping painfully against her wrist. This arrow, aimed at the spearman that circled to the left, caromed off the rock and shattered, spraying her target with splinters. He flinched and hesitated, giving Miri time to grab another arrow and draw back her bow.

The half-light air was filled with shouts and the clatter of weapons. Miri glanced at Ninshi to see her pull her sword from the body of one man, and spin almost faster than the eye could follow to grasp the shaft of a spear thrust at her. Ninshi bent and pulled, and the man staggered past. Her sword licked out, and the man fell forward screaming, the back of his legs sliced open.

Miri fumbled for another arrow, dropped it, grabbed another. She had lost track of the spearman on her left. He may have been the one Ninshi had wounded. She spun on her heel, seeking a target. There was only the guard captain left standing. There was a smear of blood on his shoulder, and the strap of his harness dangled free on one side.

Ninshi and the captain circled each other. Both of her arms were covered with blood, and her sword dripped red-black in the near-darkness. He feinted at her head, and she slipped back. His backhanded blow sliced the air. Ninshi dove forward and thrust, narrowly missing him as he twisted to one side.

They both moved back, and resumed their circling. Miri pulled back her bow and let fly. The arrow skidded off of the ground in front of the guard captain, and clattered harmlessly sideways against his boots. He gritted a smile at Miri's poor marksmanship, then looked down with the same amused smile at Ninshi's sword where it was thrust into his chest. He toppled backwards off the blade and slid to the ground.

There was a clatter of hooves, and Miri looked up to see the men with the horses riding away. She looked for an arrow to shoot after them, but felt Ninshi's hand on her arm. "Let them go. They will tell the others and they will no longer seek us."

Ninshi's face was tear-streaked, and a cut on her jaw bled slowly down her neck. She turned away to check the man she had wounded, but he had bled out and was dead.

Miri helped Ninshi as she gathered the dead men, stripped them, and laid them in a row at the bottom of the river bed twenty paces or so away from the rocks. As she removed the sandals from one she found herself suddenly unable to remember how to untie a simple knot, and unable to see for the tears. She sat shaking and crying silently for a time. When she had wept herself out, she found Ninshi at her side, holding out a piece of tunic from one of the men, the cotton soaked in water. Miri took it gratefully, and washed the tears from her face.

"You did well, child. I am proud of you. Now you must go and wait behind the rocks, for I must summon the Manthycore so that he may feed. Make no sound, and do not come back until I call you, for while he is here I will not be able to protect you, and he has a particular taste for warriors. Tomorrow or the next day we shall find a tavern, and rid ourselves of this ruby."

Miri was nearly to the rock before she realized what Ninshi had called her.

Warrior!

Hidden in the Shadows

Nothing But Our Tears

Til laid on his side facing the fire. His hands and feet were bound before him with strips of leather that cut deep into the already swollen flesh. The bandits hadn't beaten him, really, just enough to let him know that they held mastery over him. Til was too weary and discouraged to sit up. It was so much easier to stay where they had flung him.

The fire against the night blinded him to anything beyond it, which was just as well. Right now the bandits were no doubt dividing the spoils of their treachery with the caravan guards who were their accomplices. Nearly all that his family owned, the sum of his patrimony, was bundled in the bales they unloaded that nightfall as they made camp. That dawn Til was the owner of it all. This sunset he was just another portion of the loot.

It was temporary, though. His uncle had negotiated his ransom with the bandits. In two or three days he would return and Til would be free, though now quite poor. Still, his family had been traders for generations. This was not the first such setback, nor would it be the last. At least the family had the wisdom to keep a small cache of valuable goods in each city they traded in for just such occurrences.

His keeper snored on a log behind him. Til could tell by the height that the snores came from that the erstwhile guard slept sitting up. The bandits were wise enough to keep good watch, perhaps because they spent at least half of their time as caravan guards. No sense in going to all the trouble of setting up the theft of the caravan just to lose it to other bandits.

Til managed to gather enough strength to shift his face away from the fire a bit. His front was too hot, while his backside was quite cold, as were his shoulder and hip where they rested on the stony ground of the mountain pass camp. He could have asked for a covering. Even if his guard were so inclined to give him one, he would pay for the gift with a kick or two for waking him. Til's ribs were already tender.

He wriggled around to free his hip from a stone which was stabbing at it from the ground. As he did his keeper's snoring stopped. Til froze, and cringed in anticipation at the kick he knew would follow. Instead, he heard a strange gurgle and thunk. A cabbage-sized lump flew past, trailing hair. It bounced on the ground between Til and the fire, and rolled to its edge. Warm rain pattered down on him, rain with the coppery smell of blood. The hair caught fire, and in its brief flare he recognized the profile of his keeper, now no longer attached to his body.

Til tensed, prepared to cry out, knowing that the next blow would fall on him. A warm, wet hand clamped over his mouth, foul with the taste of fresh blood. At the same time a voice breathed into his ear. "Be still."

It was the voice of the strange woman who had joined the caravan the day before. The one who dressed as a man and carried a man's weapons. Til had assumed that she was dead, or raped, or both, along with her daughter.

"I need your help. Do you understand?" Her accent was strange, though she spoke the language of Khett clearly.

Til nodded. She lifted the hand from his mouth.

"I cannot," Til whispered. "I am hostage to my uncle's return. He will be back in a three-day with my ransom."

"Your uncle has sold you for his freedom. He lied. He will not return, not in a three-day; not ever." Til shook his head in denial, though he knew as she spoke that it was true. No love had ever been lost between them in spite of the bond of blood. His uncle had resented Til's father before him, just as he resented Til now. Here was his chance to collect the caches in the cities all the way to Carcamesh. Either he would use the goods to start his own trade, or more likely set up as a merchant in one of the greater cities like Ur or Babylon, where their family was unknown and none would think to question his fortune. Til's eyes blurred with tears, and the little hope he had left faded to ash.

"I tried to warn him, when we joined you. I could see that the guards intended betrayal. I misjudged, though. I thought they would wait until we were through the mountains before turning and we would be safely away. You would think that I would know more of betrayal." She snorted, and there was a brief silence.

"Help me," she whispered in that strange, harsh voice. "I must free the girl. You will want your goods."

Til coughed a bitter laugh. Of course her daughter was still alive. She would fetch a decent price. Unlike her mother, she was young and fair. Not that her mother was old, but she was far from fair. Til's uncle had whispered laughingly when he first spied her, striding into their camp. Her hair was plaited back and oiled, which only served to better show her scarred, weathered visage. "Look at that sword," he whispered. It was heavy and oddly curved, sheathed in hair-covered animal hide. "It clearly is for the protection of her daughter's virtue, if daughter that be. Her own virtue is as safe as any could be," his uncle had said.

Til hissed into the darkness. "Free me, and we will both flee. There are too many of them. Both your daughter and my goods are lost."

"No. They are not. We will free the girl. You will take her to the ridge, up there. I will call you back when all is done. If I fall, then flee if you like."

Til's uncle also had said she was mad, to walk into a camp like that and expect to travel with the caravan east through the mountain pass from Khett to the cities of the plain. He asked her for payment for their protection. She laughed without humor, said something about protecting them, but paid. Til had no idea how she had escaped when this evening the guards welcomed the rest of their gang into camp with open arms, but her daughter had not been so lucky. They bound her when they bound him, but he had not seen her since.

Mad, his perfidious uncle said. He was right. But perhaps it was a madness that would serve.

"How?" he asked.

She cut his bonds with quick motions. "I will kill the sentries, those who remain. This will reduce their numbers to eight. When I am done, I will distract them. When I do, cut into the tent where she is held: the black one in center of camp. Take this." She handed him a small, sharp knife. He grasped it in fingers that tingled with returning strength. He recognized it as one that until moments ago hung at the belt of his keeper.

"Understand?" He nodded.

"Good. Take her to the ridge. Wait. When I am done, you may reclaim your goods."

"How? What about the bandits?"

"They will be dead."

"Dead?"

"Yes. I will kill them all. Do not come back down until I have finished. The girl will tell you when."

Til nodded. She vanished into the darkness.

Kill them all? Mad!

He got up, moved around to the rear of the tent. He could hear the erstwhile guards laughing and talking on the other side, by the big central fire. Behind the tent, it was dark, shadowed from the fires. He was to take the girl to the ridge.

The girl. This was the real reason Til hadn't just bolted for the ridge. Even his uncle, who had no eye for women, had seen she was lovely. She was young, perhaps fourteen or fifteen summers, younger than Til by only a handful of years. She had stood beside her companion with the same bold confidence, but on her the boldness was a garment of beauty rather than a warning of danger. "Priestesses, I'll warrant. Or some sort of warrior maids," his uncle had whispered. "There are many strange cults in Khett. They believe there are a thousand gods. Plenty of room there for someone like them."

Til had listened with less than half an ear. His eyes were filled by her face, her dark eyes, her raven hair, plaited like her companion's, but thicker, darker, and more lustrous. She was taller than her companion by half a hand. Willowy, with a quick smile, which she flashed when she saw him watching.

Twice through the day he had managed to speak with the girl. Both times he was smitten by her liveliness and obvious spirit. Perhaps it was just the contrast with her companion, however, who stalked along beside her, unsmiling and impervious to charm or conversational opening.

"What took you to Khett?" he had asked.

"We were seeking herbs." So they were priestesses, then.

"And why do you leave?"

She laughed, flashed him a mischievous smile. "We found them."

Even her accent was charming. Til's traveler's eye had recognized her as Ibaru, a tribe from the far south near where the Great Northbound River linked the Two Kingdoms, ruled by the pharaohs. Many of her tribe were in servitude there. Sometimes they were traded this far north, but it was still unusual to see them. It was very unlikely that her companion was her mother, at least by birth. She had called her companion Nin, which meant lady, or sometimes Ninshi, which may have been either a name or a shortened title.

The girl's name was Miri. And right now she was held, no doubt still bound, in the tent before him. His tent, or it was before it was taken from him, made of cloth from a land beyond the cities of the plain, beyond the great steppes far away to the east. The idea of cutting it grieved his merchant's heart, but there was nothing for it if he was to enter and exit silently.

He could just run. With luck he could overtake his uncle, and with the knife as a meager weapon, could perhaps persuade him to reconsider his treachery. If indeed he had betrayed him, and was not just doing as he had promised.

He thumbed the curved edge of the knife. The bronze was sharp. He could fight with it, if it came to that. Better, though, would be to wait for whatever disturbance the madwoman made, grab the girl, and go. If he was quick enough, he might even beat his uncle to the cache in Kadesh, and so at least start again as a trader.

On the other side of the tent someone shouted, a deep bellow of rage. Instantly there was a babble of voices and a trample of feet toward the central fire. Til worked quickly, stabbing the small knife into the fabric of the tent an arm's length from the ground, and worried the edge down. Carefully he pulled the sides of the slit apart, and peered through.

Carpets and animal hides lined the floor of the tent. In the center was an unlit fire circle. Dim light from the fire outside flickered in through the tent's open flaps. Directly before him, not an arm's length away, was the bundled form of the girl. She lay facing him, bound as he had been. Her face was hidden in the shadow, but he knew it was her.

She knew him, too. Silently, she thrust her hands forward, and he cut her bonds. She bent at the middle, and thrust her feet through the slit he had made. He sliced through the cord which held her legs together, thrilling for a moment at the brush of the back of his hand against the bare skin of her calves. She wriggled feet first through the slit, scooting on her buttocks until she sat beside him behind the tent. He motioned to the back of the camp.

She shook her head no. For a sinking moment he thought that she was refusing to leave her companion. He started to hiss something but stopped when she bent forward and started rubbing her ankles vigorously. Of course! She couldn't run if her feet slept.

Nervously he looked around. There was still a great deal of shouting going on in the center of the camp, but it was only a matter of time before someone noticed that they were missing. He motioned her to hurry. She nodded and rose to a crouch. Together they scuttled into the darkness that ringed the camp, outside its fires' glow.

The ridge was their best path, the quickest way to be away from the camp. On the other side was a loop of the road. He led the girl over a small hillock and around to the slope up. Their footing was unsure in the gloom, but the clear half moon lit their path somewhat and the fear of capture overcame any timidity they might have felt about running about in the dark.

Below the shouting had subsided a bit. Side by side, they crawled to the edge and looked down into the camp. Til stared, amazed.

The bandit guards were gathered around the fire in front of the tent. On the far side of the fire, two figures circled, weapons drawn. Til recognized the taller one as one of the steppe-dweller brothers they had hired in Hatt, armed with a spear. The other brother was nowhere to be seen.

The other figure was the madwoman. In one hand she held her heavy-tipped sword, its bronze flashing in the firelight. In the other hand she gripped a human head, swinging by its long hair. She turned at a feint from the spearman, and in the change of light Til recognized, even from a distance, that the head belonged to the other brother.

Til was no warrior, but he had seen many fights, both bandit attacks and in the arena. To his eye, the madwoman was as good as dead. She returned none of the steppe man's spear thrusts. Twice she used the flat of her sword to block his lunges. Other than that her defense consisted of ducking and slipping to either side. Her motions seemed sluggish, unsure. The crowd around them shouted taunts and cheered each thrust the steppe man made.

Til tugged at the girl's sleeve. "We must go," he whispered. "I will protect you from here, but we must go."

Miri pulled him back down. "We must wait for her," she hissed.

"You don't see. She is overmatched. There is nothing we can do for her. Save yourself seeing this."

"Wait," she hissed back.

Then the girl did something that sent cold down Til's back, and he realized that she was as mad as the woman below. She sat up, cupped her hands, and shouted.

"Ninshi, I am safe!" she cried.

Til almost leapt up and fled right then. All that kept him from running was a perverse desire to see the consequences of their shared madness. That and the fear that the girl would simply follow him, shouting and pointing, until they both were recaptured. Better to sneak away, be gone before the girl knew it.

He started to ease back, when a motion below caught his eye. The madwoman leapt into the air, straight up, and shouted something. As she rose, she whirled the head by its hair and flung it like a sling into the face of the steppe man before her. He flinched back, and had time to cry out once before his head joined that of his brother on the ground.

The remaining bandits roared, and rushed forward. The madwoman was trapped by a circle of angry, armed men, bent on cutting her down.

Except she wasn't there.

As they closed on her, Ninshi feinted left, and with unbelievable speed, ducked under the outstretched arm of her nearest attacker. As she moved behind him, her sword licked out, and he screamed and dropped his sword. He fell over backward, the back of his legs sliced apart at the knees. The man next to him was only half turned, mouth gaping open in shock and astonishment, when she dove, thrusting as she passed. He fell atop the body of the steppe man, tangling the feet of two others who ran forward with spears.

Kill them all, the madwoman had said. Mad she might be, but Til had seen nothing like this. Ninshi moved so fast as to seem sometimes in two places, leaping, whirling, and cutting. As she fought, she sang, croaking out the words to an old song in her strange, harsh voice.

"Love is the slayer, love the betrayer,
Love the blood drinker, slayer of men."

The bandits fell over each other, first in their attempts to get to her, and finally in their vain attempts to get away. The last two stood back-to-back amidst the heaped bodies of their companions. One of them shouted defiance as the madwoman slowly circled, looking for an opening. She flicked blood from her sword at them, and they flinched, but didn't drop their guards. One, the taller, was armed with spear and a round shield, the other with the sickle-sword favored by the Khettites.

Ninshi shouted something in a language Til didn't recognize, and the taller man, a Nubian, shouted something back in the same tongue, but stood his ground.

It didn't matter.

It was over in an instant. Til wasn't even sure what happened. One moment Ninshi circled, taunting, the next she was a blur of motion, somehow between them, swinging her sword in a great arc that barely paused as it sliced through one man, and ended in the chest of the other. The sickle sword fell clattering on a rock, broken in two.

She stepped back, rocked her sword free from the dead man, wiped it on his hair, sheathed it and bent down. She moved first one body then another into a straight line, side by side, and stripped them of clothing.

Til just sat there for a moment, stunned. Then like a great rush of water falling from a mountainside, he realized that he was no longer poor, that what was his was his again. He leapt up, started to run down to embrace the madwoman, to reclaim his goods, to offer her reward.

Miri yanked him down again, with unexpected strength. "Do you wish to perish, then?" she hissed. "Be still, and silent, if you value your life."

He started to protest, but one look at her face told him that she was serious, deadly serious. He watched as the woman below, Ninshi, finished arranging and stripping corpses. Three times, she disappeared into the darkness, only to reappear moments later with a corpse over her shoulder, each of them bigger than she by half or more. She must be incredibly strong, Til thought.

He was starting to grow impatient. What was she doing? Was it some kind of ritual?

She stood back from the line of naked corpses, and pulled something on a thong from around her neck and held it up.

It seemed to Til that the world wavered and danced, like the lines of heat that rise up from the baking stone floor of the eastern deserts in the summer mid-day. At the same time, pain stabbed into his head, from his eyes and from his ears. Through agonized tears he saw a shadow form beside the line of bodies and solidify into the form of a lion. But this lion was unlike any other, standing man-high at the shoulder, with a tail that curved above its back like a scorpion's sting. From its sides sprouted great wings.

Til realized that he had seen lions like this, lions of stone, but never had he thought to see one in the flesh. It was the great beast. The devourer of men.

It was the Manthycore.

If Til's bladder had been full, it would have emptied. Pain was forgotten. His goods were forgotten. The treachery of his uncle, the beauty of the girl beside him, all forgotten. All that remained now was fear and growing horror.

Ninshi cried out in a lilting tongue, incongruous in her harsh rasping voice. The Manthycore's lion visage changed and flowed, became something nearer the face of a man. It rumbled a reply in the same strange, musical language.

Nishi peered forward transfixed, mesmerized by something beyond the fire that Til could not see, oblivious to the great beast before her as it dipped its head, features flowing into fangs and great jaws, and started to feed.

Something broke loose in Til's spirit, and he scrambled backward in panic.

Miri's body slammed into him, rolling him over. She scrambled atop him, held him down. They rolled back and forth in the dirt and rocks, Til too frightened to cry out, until they both collapsed in a panting heap.

"Be still," she whispered. "It will be over soon, but while she is like this she sees only her lover, and cannot protect us from the beast."

Til's mind found its way back from whatever place it had fled. He realized that she lay atop him, her face close to his. He could feel her breath on his cheek. A strand of her hair had been knocked loose from its plait. It draped across her face, stuck there by perspiration and dirt. The light which shone up from the fire below was uncertain, but in its pale glow she was beautiful.

He raised his head slightly, feeling her heartbeat against his.

"Miri!" Ninshi's harsh voice shouted from below. "It is finished."

Miri lifted her head, started to rise. Then with a movement every bit as rapid as any made by the woman below, she swooped down, pressed her lips against his for a single heartbeat, and sprang up. She reached down for his hand, helped him to his feet.

"We are here!" she cried.

Together they stumbled back down into the camp. Til had a moment of dread as he walked into the full light of the fire, but the Manthycore was a fastidious eater. Except for a few splashes of blood and the pile of clothes and weapons to one side, there was no sign of the ghastly feast.

Til noticed the madwoman staring at him. For a moment the fear returned, and then he realized that he was still holding Miri's hand. He dropped it. Something like a flicker of amusement crossed her scarred, weathered face.

"This boy," she said. "Was he brave?"

Miri grabbed his hand, squeezed it. "He was very brave. He even offered to protect me."

"Good. The mountains are a dangerous place. A woman needs a protector here."

Miri giggled. "I think you just made a joke, Ninshi."

She stalked away. "Sleep," she growled over her shoulder.

They lay together on their backs, looking at the night sky, still holding hands. Occasionally Til would start to tremble, and Miri would hold him and stroke his brow until the memory of the evening passed. They talked in whispers; as if they were afraid that whatever spell held them together might break at the sound of a word spoken aloud.

Miri told him of the madwoman, Ninshi, the woman from the songs. How after centuries of pain and murder and despair she had found a way to free herself.

"What will you do, when she is free?" asked Til.

"Then I will be free as well. I will marry I think, perhaps some rich, old, fat merchant, and live in a house with servants." She smiled, and kissed him, feathery and quick, as before.

"Why do you follow her?" he asked.

"Because when I prayed for her, she came."

"She answers prayers? Is she a goddess then?"

"No, and never suggest such to her. She does what she does for her own reasons sometimes, but she only believes in one god, and does not worship him." Miri shifted a little, so her hip fit more snugly against his. "She does what she does for the most powerful of reasons, I think."

Til nodded. "Revenge."

Miri elbowed him and snorted.

"No," she said, and kissed him. "For love."

Tricked by Fire

The Scarlet Colored Beast

I lay slumped against the wall while around me the city burned. Smoke, fatigue and pain blurred my vision. I was lost. I got turned around in the last fight and by the time I was clear of it I was here, in a part of the city I had never been. Blood from the wound in my side ran down my hip to join the pool from the body of the man who had made it. His spear was still clutched in his hand, bloodied bronze tip pointing to me like an accusation of failure.

I had come here seeking peace. What I found is what I find everywhere. Betrayal and death.

I pulled myself up. The pain made the world spin, what I could see of it. By shifting a little, I was able to get at the knife I kept in the top of my boot. I used it to cut a long strip from one of my linen leggings. I folded it over, made a pad with its end, and used the rest to tie up the wound in my side. It was narrow but deep, a killing wound. The spearman had known his business. He just hadn't known his adversary.

I would not die from this. The lifetimes of wearing the broken-tooth talisman that was the symbol and the cause of my bondage ensured that I would heal. That is, I would heal if I survived the day, which seemed less and less likely.

As I finished binding my wound, I heard the clatter of sandals on the hardened earth of the street. Through the smoke, I glimpsed the shapes of a handful of men as they ran past. They carried spears and small oval shields. Either they were not looking for me or they missed me in the haze. Their forms vanished from sight less than twenty paces away and the sound of their feet was soon lost to the sounds of a dying city: screams in the distance, somewhere the clash and shouts of men fighting and the roar of buildings consumed by flame.

I pushed myself upright, using the half wall behind me for support. My back scraped against the rough clay bricks. As I rose, the remains of the legging on my right side spiraled off into a heap at my feet. The trailing end landed atop the head of one of the three other men I had fought here. Killing them had kept me busy enough that their compatriot had managed to thrust his spear deep into my side before I was able to kill him, too.

I stumbled forward, using the wall as a support. I could stand now, though the pain in my side kept me from being able to draw a full breath.

A burning building across from me illuminated the street. I had no idea which direction I had come from. I did know that it would be a while before I could fight, so I chose to go the opposite direction of the soldiers who had just passed.

I stumbled around for a while, unsure of my direction. I needed to find the temple, near the center of this city. There I hoped to find Miri, my adopted daughter and companion this last handful of years. I also hoped to find the concoction of herbs we had gathered at such difficulty and danger over that time. We had brought them here to Aratta to have them brewed together by the ancient priests of the city.

At last I found the edge of a well or a cistern. I knelt down, brushed scum and wet ash from the surface, and thrust my head into the water, drinking deep gulps of it. It was brackish, tainted with ash. After a time I pulled back, shook water from my face and gasped. My braid had fallen over my shoulder as I drank, but the heavy oil it was coated with caused the moisture to bead and run off in slow dirty dollops. I stood up, stronger now.

I looked around. To my left I could see the bulk of the temple, the white of its sloped sides marred here and there by slicks of blood from the bodies of priests and soldiers left in my trail down. Miri would meet me there, if she was not at the caravansary where I had left her, and if she still lived. Painfully, I started in that direction.

We had waited for nine days before the Hierarch, as they called the High Priest here, would see me. I have the patience of centuries, but my companion Miri was barely twenty summers old, and the time weighed heavily on her. I ate and slept, and practiced with my weapons. She paced, pestered locals for gossip, or bothered the caravansary keeper with unreasonable demands for food, drink or entertainment.

At last they came, two priests and four guards. One of the priests was obviously of great importance, as both the caravansary keeper and the guards seemed cowed by his presence. It was he who spoke. "The great Hierarch has consented to see you. He wishes to hear your tale first hand, and to see the talisman you claim to carry." He was tall, with a shaven head, but his voice might have come from a child, whispery and light.

We walked through the Camel Gate into the city. It was the closest to the temple of the city's five gates, and in this part of the city at least, the sight of the priests with their shaven heads and flowing robes elicited little notice.

"That one there, the younger one," Miri whispered. "He is Tul-Adan, the deputy to the Hierarch. It is said that they disagree often, but because Tul-Adan is a younger son of the king of Uruk, the Hierarch endures him."

I looked at her, surprised. "How do you know this?" I whispered back.

"Gossip," she said. "*My* time at that dreadful caravansary was not wasted." She grinned at me.

"Yes," I replied sourly. "I am certain that the latest news about the domestic quarrels of the local shopkeepers and favored methods of beer brewing will come in quite handy." Her grin widened.

"Yet," I admitted, "this is good to know."

As we drew closer, the temple seemed to grow. It was built of clay brick, rather than stone, so it was not nearly as tall as the great monuments of the Pharaohs I had seen many years ago in my travels, or even similar ziggurats in some of the cities between the rivers, but it was impressive enough. The steps up its staggered sides and the platform at the top seemed to be stone, though, and as we came still closer, it could be seen that they were worn with the use of centuries. The whole structure was covered with some sort of whitewash, clean and bright, so that it gleamed in the afternoon sun. While perhaps a bit smaller than its counterparts elsewhere, the temple was still by far the tallest building in the city.

We were led through a low gate into a large courtyard, paved with whitewashed brick and lined with fruit trees laden with not yet ripe pomegranates, pears, olives and apples. We walked to the far end, to the front of a low building, and were bade to sit on a stone bench. The two priests vanished into the building, leaving us with the guards, who stood one at each corner, as if they expected us to bolt at any moment, but were unsure of the direction we might take.

The guards were oddly dressed, for soldiers, though well armed with long bronze-headed spears and heavy single-bladed bronze axes. Few other than the very rich or nobles wore much in the way of armor, and on most soldiers it was unusual to see much more than a few bronze disks or strips sewn onto a leather harness. They were bare-chested and kilted in white linen. Perhaps in this place soldiers were seldom called upon to fight.

After a short wait, the door to the building we were facing opened. From it issued a procession of shaven-headed priests, all wearing the same flowing robes as our escort had worn. They spread in a line across the front of the building, and from their midst came a tiny stooped figure. He looked old enough that his shiny pate may have been from nature rather than razor.

I rose to my feet, motioning Miri to do the same. He waved us down, and when we sat, came and sat between us. "I am an old man," he explained in a voice still strong in spite of his apparent years. "I prefer we sit."

I said nothing, waiting. After a time, he nodded. "May I see it?" he asked finally.

I pulled the broken-tooth talisman by its leather thong from where it rested against my breast. He leaned forward, peered intently at its dark stained surface, gently poked a time or two with one shaking finger, then motioned for me to put it away.

"It is an ill-looking thing, is it not? Fitting, I think, for what it is, and for what it represents. Here then is the end of a tale that I have heard all of my life. But I know only of the first part of the tale. You must tell me the ending. How did you come by it, and what is it you want from us?"

"There was an old man," I began. "Dressed as you are, I think, but the passing of years makes me unsure."

"How many years?"

"Perhaps six hundred. Perhaps more. It is difficult to keep track. Part of the talisman's curse is that it preserves, unaging."

He drew in harsh breath through withered gums. "Yet not unchanging, I see," he said, peering at my scarred face.

I did not look away. Once, when I was a girl, I may have been beautiful. None would ever call me that again.

"No," I said, and began my story. I talked until dusk, telling of how the boy I loved and I had come upon an old man on the road, dressed as the Hierarch was, in the midst of an ambush by bandits. We had come to his aid, but had been too late to save him. With his dying breath he told us of a great treasure and a foul Beast, the Manthycore, and gave us a talisman in the form of a great broken tooth, which he said could compel the Beast. But instead of commanding the Beast, the Beast commanded us.

Besides unnaturally long life, the talisman had made me impossibly resilient, and the long centuries passed in murder and betrayal.

Then I heard of seven rare herbs, planted after the great deluge by the servant of Enki. The *Shappatu*, when mixed correctly, could compel the obedience of any beast, small or great. We had journeyed to Khett to find them, and after great hardship were able to gather all seven. But on our return, we learned that the wise man who told me of them had died, and that the priests of the local cult had burned his library. For the next few years we wandered from one purported place of wisdom to another, until one night at a campfire we had heard a song about the goddess Innana, and how she had moved her temple from the city of Aratta to Uruk because she would not abide a beast who dwelt there, a beast who could take any form, but most often took the shape of a great lion, with wings of an eagle and the body of a bull. Songs were often false, but equally as often contained some truth. There were songs about me, too, most of them terribly wrong. Yet I lived and walked upon the earth. So I thought there might be something to be learned in the city of Aratta, from the priests there, who in the song were able to command the birds of the air and the beasts of the field.

Through this long story the old man sat silent, asking only an occasional question for clarification. When I was finished I dried my face, for though my story is old to me, my grief and the burden of many lives taken is fresh upon me at each telling.

Then it was the old man's turn to talk. "This is a story known only to a few here, guarded as one of our great secrets. But as you are a part of the tale, I think it fit that you hear of it.

"Many, many lives of men ago, this temple and these priests served the goddess Innana, and her servant the Fire. We grew prosperous and powerful in our service, and for centuries we were unchallenged even by the great kings of the cities between the rivers, or the populous peoples to the east. In our prosperity and pride we grew arrogant, and grew to think little of those we served. One day a wanderer came who told the then Hierarch of an even greater power, one that if wielded by one possessing sufficient will could command even the gods. For a talent of silver, the wanderer promised to lead the Hierarch to a cave in the mountains, where a great beast had been imprisoned since shortly after the great deluge. Once there, he would give the Hierarch a talisman that would command the beast.

"In his pride, the Hierarch never thought to ask if the talisman could command such a great power, why the wanderer was willing to sell it for such a small price. True, an entire talent of silver is no small amount, but if one were able to command such a beast, what need would you have of precious metal?

"The wanderer led the Hierarch and a large number of his followers into the mountains to the north. There they came to a small cave sealed with brick and strange writings. The wanderer handed the Hierarch the talisman, but when he turned again to ask how it might be used, the wanderer had vanished, unpaid.

"He ordered the sealed cave open, and his soldiers knocked down the ancient bricks, which were so old that they crumbled to dust as each was thrown aside. When it was open, he ordered his men inside. Before they could enter, there was a roar of triumph, and a great beast leapt forth. It was larger than a bull or bear, and had great wings. It fell upon them, devouring each in turn, until only the Hierarch remained. What it then told him, for it could speak in the tongue of men, was known only to the Hierarch himself.

"Humbled and afraid, he made his way back to Aratta. Here he found that at what must have been the very instant of his opening of the cave, the goddess had fled to Uruk. Whether she left in fear or in wrath is unknown. She left only this sacred talisman of the Fire, now unusable without her presence." He raised his left hand to show me a small golden torque about his wrist, from which dangled the image of a tiny flame made of gold.

"Soon after, the sacred herbs with which we commanded the birds of the air and the beasts of the field all withered and died, unable to grow here so far from their natural home far to the west without her nurturance. And the Hierarch, who had once been so proud, now resolved to abdicate his position. He determined to wander the earth in poverty until he found either the herbs to compel the Beast, or until he had found some other way to free us of its curse. For curse it was, commanding him to bring it freshly killed men for it to feed upon. Though it was perfectly able to hunt for itself, it preferred its meat to be brought to it.

"I believe it was the Hierarch you met upon the road, who set you upon the long path that has led you here. I am sorry, my child, for what the foolishness of one man of my order has brought you. But I think, if as you say, you have found the sacred herbs, the *Shappatu*, that perhaps at long last there will be an end to this tale. Bring them here, in the morning, and we shall see if the old lore is still good for something other than boring young acolytes to tears."

"We must have a plan," I said. "I do not trust these priests. There is something here that I do not understand."

Miri snorted. "You do not trust anyone, Ninshi."

I hesitated. "Not so. I trust you."

She peered at me suspiciously through the dim morning light of the caravansary's courtyard. "Yes Ninshi. I know you do. But for you to actually say it means that there is something you are going to tell me, something I doubt I will like."

I nodded. "I both hope and fear that this will be our final time together. If today goes as I wish, I will be finally free of my service to the Manthycore. Or it could be that the priests will simply take the herbs, and kill me."

Miri stared at me in disbelief. "Kill you? Is that possible?"

"Of course. Like any mortal, no matter how fierce or long-lived, I can be killed. True, long practice and experience makes me formidable, and the power of the talisman prevents any but the most dire wound from ending my life, as well as protecting me against any sorcery save its own. But I am mortal, born of woman, just as you are, and in the end I will return to dust."

"But not today." She smiled weakly.

"Perhaps not. I hope today to compel the Manthycore to free me and my lover. There are many possible outcomes to that action. Most involve destruction and death. I want you to wait here. Should something unforseen happen, I want you to go to Til the merchant, in Carcamesh. He will take care of you, perhaps even marry you."

"I will not leave you here," she hissed. "Not without knowing what happens to you, not without knowing that you have succeeded, or died."

There was a pounding at the gate of the caravansary, and shouted orders. I rose to my feet. "Stay here. Wait for my return. If something happens here, and it seems safer to do so, meet me at the temple. But I would prefer that if it comes to that, that you go on to Carcamesh."

She bowed her head, perhaps to hide her tears. "I will wait here until noon."

It was the best I would get. I turned to meet the younger priest we had met yesterday, and his escort, and together we walked through the gate and through the waking city to the temple.

The old priest spoke as he ground and mixed. "There is no magic here, no prayer or incantation needed. The seven herbs of the *Shappatu* need only to be mixed in the right combination. Enki wished for the concoction to be simple. You see, after the deluge, there were only a very few men to carry on, and it was important that they be able to harness the beasts to rebuild the world. They had lost the power to compel them after the fall of First Man, and could no longer invoke the Name of the Creator, save in supplication. The legends say that each beast must consume the mixture, but in truth it is a balm, to be spread across the centers of thought, the forehead, heart and right hand of the one who seeks to compel obedience. Against lesser beasts such as lions or camels, or say a bear, a full day's service may be obtained. Against a great beast, such as the one you serve, only one task may be given, and that in great peril. For truly, it was not the greater beasts it was intended for. Often, the greater beasts were not originally beasts at all, but have chosen to take that form. Those who have can be compelled only because once having taken the form of beasts, they also assume part of the beast's nature. I ask that once I have mixed this, that you use it far from our city, as we have already been cursed in the past by the presence of that fell beast. His very presence was enough to cause the goddess Inanna to forsake us, and move her temple to the west."

"Is this not an opportunity for us to return to Aratta the favor of the Goddess?" The younger priest said in his whispery voice. The sun glinted from his shaven head. "If indeed it was the bringing here of the talisman so long ago that caused her to leave."

The Hierarch shook his head. "To do so would mean summoning the Fire, her servant and precursor. I fear the danger of that would outweigh the possibility of Her return. And at any rate, the Beast would have to be either destroyed or driven forth by the Fire, and neither outcome would be certain."

The younger priest started to say something more, but stopped himself. He glanced across the temple platform where we stood to the great stone bowl of oil from which flame steadily flickered. At its round base was carved the figure of a lizard, long tail looping around to drape over its neck.

The platform itself stood at the very top of the temple. It was about twenty paces across, and like the rest of the building was covered in whitewash. At the center stood an altar around which we were gathered, the two priests and I. The guards waited on the steps just out of sight below the edge of the temple platform.

"But Master, don't you see? Here is what we have prayed so long for, our return to the greatness of our fathers. With the power of the Fire and the Beast, we can return the goddess to here from Uruk. We could order the riches and the power of all the kings of all the cities of the earth to flow to here. From here we could rule everything."

The old priest shook his head sadly. "It is thought like that that caused our downfall, all these many years ago. No, we must not tamper with what we do not understand."

"I expected no less from you, old man," hissed the younger priest. From his robe, he drew a dagger and plunged it into the chest of the Hierarch.

"Guards!" he shouted. "She has slain the Hierarch! Seize her!" He threw the bloodied dagger at my feet.

My sword flew into my hand, but they were too many and I had no place to run. A dozen spears pointed at my throat, and a dozen more were at my back. Hope and the treachery of the priest had betrayed me. I was the mistress of betrayal, and yet, when hope was dangled before me, I seemed to lose that final edge of suspicion. At least I had sense enough leave Miri behind.

My sword clattered to the pavement, and they prodded me back into a corner.

"Keep her here," ordered the young priest. "Half of you go to the caravansary where her companion waits, and bring her here." They clattered down the steps.

"The old man may have been right. It may be too dangerous to summon both the Beast and the Fire. Should the Manthycore prevail, the goddess may never come. But what if the Fire were to slay the bearer of the Manthycore's talisman and destroy it? Could the Beast ever again be summoned?" He stalked over and glared at me. "Could it?"

"I don't know."

"I think you do. And I think in a moment we both will know." He walked back to the altar, bent down to the small huddled corpse of the Hierarch and pulled from his wrist the golden torque with its dangling flame of gold. Behind the altar, he stood for a moment, then with two fingers of his left hand dipped into the chalice and smeared the concoction on his forehead, breast and the back of his right hand.

He turned to the bowl of fire behind him. He held the dangling charm over the flame, and chanted in a language unknown to me. For several minutes, we stood there as he chanted. Then he turned, and holding the charm over the altar shouted, "Come forth!"

For several heartbeats, nothing happened. The flame from the bowl flared and rose. From it flew a small figure made of flame, lizard-shaped as the likeness carved around the base of the stone bowl. It was perhaps two hands across, no more.

The young priest's cry of triumph was drowned by the gasps of fear from the soldiers surrounding me. It was bright, almost too bright to look at, and it droned a high-pitched whine, like the sounds of the clouds of insects found at river's edge at dusk. It darted around the altar for a moment, first higher, then lower, as if searching for something. Then it stilled, and floated an arm's length from the young priest at the level of his eyes.

The priest looked directly at the Fire. Its scarlet light reflected in his eyes, so bright that it seemed from where I stood as if it came from within the priest himself, and that the Fire was the reflection. "This I command," he cried in his small whispery voice. "I command you to destroy the talisman of the Beast and its bearer."

"Manling, you cannot." The voice of the Fire was high-pitched and song-like. "You have already commanded me once, in summoning me here, without the bidding of my mistress or the proper use of the charm. What I owe you now is not obedience. What I owe you now is your reward."

The small lizard spread its wings, and the flame that surrounded it flared brightly. It rose up and then plunged directly into the open mouth of the priest. For a few terrible moments, he thrashed and gurgled choked screams, and then he was still, his robes emitting black oily smoke as he burned. Flames flickered from his empty eyes and his open mouth. From it flew the Fire, larger than before, and it danced upon his body, consuming whatever it touched.

My sword. I needed my sword. I could fight with any tool given, or none at all, but with my sword I had slain a multitude of men, beasts, spirits and demons. The spearmen who surrounded me had less than half an eye for me, staring at the body of the young priest as it was consumed by the living flame. My sword lay where I had dropped it, halfway to the altar.

I waved my arm at the nearest. "You, boy. I need your spear."

He looked at me, anger fighting fear. "My spear? You shall have it, then!"

He lunged forward, the bronze barbless tip jabbing at my vitals. I slid to the side, slapped at the haft with my right hand, caught it an arm's length beyond with my left. I turned and pulled, yanking him past me, levering the spear from his grasp. He stumbled to his knees, then slammed prone, driven by my thrust of his spear into his back. Before his companions could react, two more were dead. The others fled, either in fear of me or in fear of the Fire. Perhaps both.

Two quick steps took me to my sword. I scooped it up, and ran at the fiery creature before me. It rose from its feast to meet me. The blade of my sword rang as its bronze met the Fire's lizard-like body. The Fire was flung away by the force of the blow, and my sword jumped back in my hand as if I had struck it flat against the bole of a tree. The body of the Fire slammed against the base of the altar, cloven nearly in two. Its flame flickered, darkened, and turned blue. Its hind legs kicked, and the whining sound it had made since it was summoned ceased.

I carefully examined my blade. The bronze was scorched, but not nicked or cracked. I looked again to the corpse of the Fire. It had not been so dire. A small blue ball of fire flicked over it, then rose to where the sacred oil burned in the stone bowl behind the altar. There it joined with the flame, and was gone.

"You must..." a voice croaked. I turned to finish whichever of the spearman still had life enough to speak. Instead I was surprised to see the old priest, struggling to raise his head. I had thought him dead.

"You cannot slay it with your sword."

"Quiet, old man. I just did."

"No. Look. It rises again."

The flame over the stone bowl grew brighter, smaller, and more solid. It formed again into the shape of a lizard, this time twice as large as the two hand's span in length it had been before. I raised my sword quickly, and was barely able to strike it before it collided with me. I was hurled onto my back, skidding against the harsh brick of the temple platform. I could feel my eyebrows singe away, and the back of my hands blistering.

The Fire fell in two pieces, one to each side of me, and each piece started to flicker, as before. I rolled over, got to my knees, and scrambled over to the old priest where he lay.

"How can I kill this thing?" I rasped through dry lips.

"You cannot. Only the Beast you serve or another Great Beast can, by means of its sorcerous nature. Killing it by natural means just makes it return from the fire, stronger than before."

"Then I will use the herbs and command it to depart."

He coughed blood. It misted from his breath as he spoke. "No. Only once. No matter who, once compelled, it can never be again."

"What if I don't kill it? What will it do then?"

"It will consume the world. With each fire it starts, it will grow, becoming strong enough to slay you, and every other thing upon the earth. The Goddess could control it; none other can. It will burn and grow and destroy until there is nothing left that is green or alive, only ash." The old man coughed blood.

The flame solidified again. This time instead of rushing at me, it flitted down and away, landing in the straw roof a house on the street below. The house exploded into flame, and the Fire rose larger and brighter than before. The whining sound was clearer now. It was not a high-pitched howl, as I had thought before. No, the Fire was *singing*.

There was a clatter of steps as the soldiers returned. "There!" one of them shouted. "She has slain the Hierarch!"

I turned to tell the old priest to explain, but he was dead.

There were twenty or more of them. They drove me from the temple platform, leaving a trail of bodies and blood down the white sloping sides. More joined those who were not killed by me or by an occasional swoop of the Fire as it danced randomly across the city and set it ablaze. Sometimes I fought. Sometimes I ran. Sometimes both. Finally I was alone, wounded, half-prone against a wall as the city burned.

The caravansary was empty, burned out. The Fire had been here. So had the soldiers. Their charred bodies were strewn across the courtyard and into the road outside. Two, the farthest away from the wall, were untouched by flame. Instead, black-feathered arrows jutted from their chests. Miri had at least survived the fire, and the soldiers who remained had suffered the results of years of her practice with the bow.

I ran back through the Camel Gate into the city. The street to the temple was littered with the remains of scorched citizens, priests, and soldiers, and in several places the way was obstructed by the burning debris of collapsed buildings. Twice I came across groups of soldiers. One paid no attention to me, being occupied in trying to fight the flames in a large building with the water from a nearby well. It was a battle they looked to lose.

The other group of soldiers blocked the street, guarding what, I do not know. At my approach, they challenged me, but one of them recognized me from the temple platform and cried out something about a death goddess, and they broke and fled.

From its base, the top of the ziggurat was shrouded in smoke. I hurried up the stairs, already weary, knowing that if the cries I heard from the top were from Miri, needing my help, I would be too late, and too weak. As I topped the stairs, a gust of wind blew aside the curtain of smoke to reveal a tall young woman sitting on the altar. In one hand she held a small double curved bow, in the other a fist full of black-feathered arrows. She was not crying. She was singing.

Love is the slayer, love the betrayer
Love the blood drinker, slayer of men.
Freedom she seeks, from the binder of youth,
Freedom she seeks, so then binds men in death.

"You came." She seemed unsurprised.

"Odd place for a concert."

She shrugged. "It was the song that brought you to me in the first place. I thought if it worked once, it might again. And as you see, it did." Her cheek was smudged with soot, and her hair was singed on one side. Her dagger was thrust into her belt, and from it strings of crimson dribbled down the side of her kilt.

I snorted. She had believed from the beginning that her prayers had brought me to her, prayers to the solitary god of her small tribe. Unable to dissuade her, I had learned to ignore her.

"You are safe and whole. Good. I wish you to go, then."

"Wait," she rose from the altar. "I cannot leave you yet. Are you free, at long last?"

"Not yet, but I may be soon. You must flee. Compelled, the Manthycore's wrath may be great and I cannot promise safety to any who are near."

She started to argue, then bowed her head and nodded.

"Go there," I pointed. "Wait at the Camel Gate. I will send the young man to meet you there. Wait only until dusk."

"The young man?" she asked. "Your young man?"

"Flee," I said. "Go to Carcamesh. Marry the merchant there, what is his name?"

"You know his name."

"Yes, well." I fumbled at my waist, my eyes full of tears. "Til, the merchant. Marry him. Have many babies. Name one for me."

"A girl or a boy?"

In spite of myself, I smiled. "One of each, if you like. Here, this purse has more than enough for a dowry. Give him half, give a fourth to the young man who will meet you at the gate. Hide the rest, so that when Til beats you, you can leave him."

"He won't beat me." Now she was crying, too.

"I know. You most likely will beat him."

She reached out, grabbed my hand. "God be with you."

"Perhaps. Remember, wait only until dusk. If the young man does not show, I will have failed. If he does, take him with you to Carcamesh. He is clever, if naive. With what you give him, he will be able to make his way, perhaps as a caravan guard for your new husband."

She clasped me close, for a moment mixing her tears with mine. "God be with you, Mother." Then she whirled and sped down the stairs.

With one hand, I pulled the broken tooth talisman by its chain from where it lay against my breast. With the other, I dipped fingers in the chalice on the altar, and spread the tarry paste across my forehead, throat, and the back of my right hand as I had seen the priest do.

I held up the talisman, stared at it, focused my will.

"Come," I whispered. "Come."

The pain in my side vanished in the shadow of the pain that stabbed at my eyes, my ears and the back of my head. I staggered, but caught myself. Only once had the Beast arrived to find me on my knees. I would never let it happen again.

After a time, my vision cleared. The Manthycore had already started to dine on the corpses strewn about the altar. As he sometimes had done, he caused another mouth to form at the top of his head so he could eat and talk at the same time.

"I see that your search was successful. You are resourceful. I believe that there is none in the world but you who could have gathered the herbs of Adapa. I am of course compelled by the *Shappatu* but I warn you, there is always a price. Gilgamesh himself paid with the life of his closest friend, and then with his own. It takes great wisdom to compel such as I am, more even than strength of will, which you have."

"Then allow me to ask advice of one who has lived since before the foundations of the world were laid. Such a one should possess great wisdom indeed."

The great beast snorted, and raised his head from his ghastly feast. He turned to face me fully, his lion's face still dripping with gore. "Speak, then. I will advise."

"I have served you long and well. But during that time, these forty lives of men or more I have also striven to be free of you, and to free my love, whom you hold against my rebellion and to compel my service."

"This I know," he rumbled in a voice suitable for thunder, or a cataract of a great river. "Your thoughts are open to me, even when I sleep."

"But now, when I might finally have done the task and acquired the thing that might free at least one of us, something else has been set upon the world that may well destroy everything that lives, making freedom of any kind for either me or my love a brief and painful reward."

The Manthycore glanced over his bull's shoulder at the city burning below. "The Fire. It has been freed, no? And once free, unless stopped, it will consume until it has consumed the world and all that is upon it. From the time we came onto this earth, only his mistress could control him, and she has gone from this place. I felt its odious joy even in my slumber. As much as I enjoy destruction, it is not yet the time for this world to end. That time is for Another to decide, and there is still much to be told in the tale of men."

"So advise me. How shall I choose? Where lies wisdom?"

The Manthycore peered at me through one half-closed golden eye. "You have indeed served me for a great while, even by my years. I am compelled by the *shappattu* to obey you, but for only one command, after which in the normal course of things I would simply devour you as a penalty for imposing on me.

But because of your long service, I will not, as you have been most useful."

The beast's great tail lashed twice as it pondered. "This I will do. The Fire is an old foe of mine, once my brother, but now unbearable. In the ages before the world, before the Great Struggle, we sang together as the Creator hung the stars. After we were cast down, the arrogance of the Fire became plain, and we quarreled. That enmity remains. I will destroy him, not in service to you, but in service to myself, and because it will please me.

"As for what your command will be, that you must choose for yourself. And in exchange for my good faith, and no trickery, you must pledge something to me. Of course, whatever you command must be within my power to accomplish. And you may command only one thing. I suspect I know what that will be."

"I suspect you do." Behind the bull's back of the Manthycore I could see the Fire rise again above the rooftops, perhaps to survey its handiwork. Below it the city was ablaze. From where we stood, I could see nearly all the valley. Fully half of the buildings below burned. The Fire had grown to an enormous size, perhaps four man heights across.

"Choose quickly, then. To tarry now only means my foe is that much the stronger. I may destroy him now, but there is a limit to my power, and he grows by the minute."

I bowed my head, overcome by grief, then spoke a command and a pledge. The great Beast nodded. He crouched, unfurled his wings and leapt into the sky. His great roar was matched by the Fire's fierce song as midway over the city they met in a clash like thunder.

I turned to the young man who suddenly stood beside me. "Go that way, down the stairs. At the great fountain turn toward the river, there." I pointed.

He blinked at me, confused. My chest constricted as I looked at him. He was beautiful, as beautiful as I remembered.

"How came I here?" he asked, in the long ago tongue of my, of our! youth.

"An enchantment, but there is no time to explain. You will meet a young woman by the Camel Gate, there. She will take you to Carcamesh, where you will live out your life."

"Is she the girl I traveled here with? I remember now. She is slender, with doe eyes, skin like milk and thick hair. Is it she?"

I choked on my answer, spat ash and despair. "She is not. That one is dead."

His hopeful face fell. So young, so young! "Will you come with me?"

"No," I said. "I must wait here, where the priests and their soldiers can find me, until you are safely away, lest in hunting me they find you."

He nodded, and turned to the stair. He hesitated, then turned.

"Go!" I shouted.

"But who are you?" he asked, peering intently at my weathered and scarred face, my tired eyes, my thick and muscled torso. "Do I know you?"

"No," I lied. "Now go!"

"No," I whispered at his back as he ran down the stairs. "That one is dead."

I turned back to face the heart of the city. High above it, the Fire and the Beast roared and spun.

Below, I could see the upturned faces of a few priests and soldiers.

Time for them to think of me. I raised my sword above my head, drew breath, and let out a great shout.

Epilogue

Northern Iraq, December 2004

Zipper hated the desert, but then he hated nearly everywhere else, so it balanced out. Baghdad had truly sucked, but the money was good, and at least a fellow could find a beer now and again. Out here, guarding an oil pumping station, beer was a distant memory. The nearest town was forty-five clicks away, and filled with the sort of Hajjis that would just as soon stick a knife in you as sell you a beer, diehard followers of old Saddam.

Still, being here alive with no beer was better than being dead in Baghdad. And the money was the same, wherever in Iraq he was. Blackthorne Security paid more in a month than he could make back home in a year, and being here there was the added bonus of being able to shoot stuff.

Shooting stuff was what had gotten them in trouble, though. Zipper and Rod had gotten drunk on cheap Lebanese beer and had gone looking for trouble. They had shot up a mosque, and even with the sloppy administration of the CPA that wasn't going to wash. In order to avoid the legal scrutiny of the Army, who did not like contractors stirring things up freelance, Blackthorne had moved all six of their entire team up north until things could cool off a little.

"Yo, Zip." Zipper raised his head, looked out the flap of the tent. It was Petey, the South African dude. Zipper was more than a little afraid of Petey, who was few years older than the rest of them. When he was drunk, he would tell stories that could make your skin crawl, about the old apartheid days.

"What's up, Petey?"

"Colonel wants you. Some Hajji woman won't go away. She doesn't seem to speak English. Colonel needs you to translate. Find out what she wants."

Zipper grunted as he stood up from his cot. He reached over and grabbed his Dragonskin body armor from where it was propped against the cooler, which sadly held only warm Pepsi. All of them wore it when walking around here. They had had some trouble with the locals in the first week, but Rod had popped a couple of them, and now they were pretty much left alone except for an occasional wild shot from the hill nearby. He shrugged into it as he made his way across the graveled parking lot to the office of the pumping station where the Colonel had made his headquarters.

Zipper was fairly certain that the Colonel had never been anything more than a senior non-com in his native Canada, but Blackthorne always called each team boss Colonel, even a team as small as six. It didn't matter, he was still the boss.

It was just as hot inside the office as it was outside. There was an air conditioning unit in the window, but like everything else here in Iraq it was broken. Behind the solitary desk sat the Colonel, taller sitting down than the figure that stood before him.

She was short, even for an Iraqi, and when she turned to look at him as he came in, he saw that her face was crisscrossed with scars, and weathered by the harsh desert sun. Her hair was thick and black, braided back and tucked into her blouse. She was wearing a mismatched collection of US BDU's with a Republican Guard beret held down by a red Coca-Cola bandana. On her feet she sported new blue Nike running shoes. Slung over her shoulder was a Mac-10, and at her waist was a Bulgarian knock-off of a Glock and a large, heavy tipped machete in a worn leather sheath still bearing scraps of some grayish fur.

"Do you then speak for your Captain?" she asked. Her Arabic was accented strangely, with oddly slurred word endings.

"Yes. He is a very busy man. Unless what you desire is of great importance..."

She looked around the office, bare except for the desk and a few dented folding chairs. "Busy. Yes."

The Colonel leaned forward. "Kinda an ugly one, no? Look at those scars on her face and hands. Looks like this one may have spent some time as a guest of Saddam or his sons."

The woman nodded vigorously. "Yes, Saddam. He gathered great treasures of the past, many of which have been stolen since his fall."

Zipper's breath caught in his throat. Everyone knew that great fortunes of ancient treasure had been looted in the chaos after the fall of Baghdad. There were rumors of guys who had found single, pocketable items that were worth hundreds of thousands of dollars. And of others who had made deals with Iraqis to ship larger pieces home, making them rich.

"She says something about loot, Colonel, about museum stuff."

The Colonel stood up, towering over the small woman in front of him. "Ask her where. Ask her how much."

"Great treasure, very dangerous, long journey, bad company," she said in her slurred Arabic. Zipper translated.

"Great treasure?" asked the Colonel, and smiled.

Writing in the Bronze Age

Bonus—a look at the author's experiences.

No, this is not about half-deciphered cuneiform on dusty clay tablets, ancient scrolls or mysterious etchings on the walls of long-ruined temples in some far-away place. Well, maybe just a little, but that is only a part of it. Mostly it is about writing stories set in the Bronze Age, along with a few examples of research, and at the gentle suggestion of the editor, a quick run-down of how the book you are holding came to pass. Sort of like the bonus features on a DVD, without the blooper reel.

Let's start by defining the Bronze Age. To be specific, the Mesopotamian Bronze Age, as that is the era dealt with in *The Servant of the Manthycore.* Different parts of the world had different beginnings and ends to their Bronze Ages, with Europe's continuing longer, and many parts of Africa skipping right from Neolithic to Iron. A lot of this had to do with the availability of tin, which along with copper is one of the two ingredients of bronze. Europe and the British Isles had a ready supply, and so the use of bronze continued for several hundred years longer than in Mesopotamia, which had very little. The Mesopotamian Bronze Age is usually dated from about 3500 B.C. to about 1100 B.C. or about 2400 years, and most likely would have continued longer except for the little understood "Bronze Age Collapse" which so disrupted trade that what little tin was available for bronze making was unobtainable.

The stories that make up *The Servant of the Manthycore* take place through the middle and into the late Bronze Age, from about 2200 B.C. to around 1560 B.C. This was the period of the great city-states, of Babylon, Ur, Nineveh and Assur. The world's first empires were formed, codes of law were established and published, and astrology was beginning to morph into astronomy, along with the attendant rise in mathematics. With weights and measures more standardized, and roads protected by local kings and empires, trade flourished, along with nearly all of the things we associate with civilized life.

Including literature. Gilgamesh, the world's first known literary character (and the first Sword and Sorcery character in history!) was the biggest star of ancient times. The earliest Sumerian versions of his story date from as early as 2150 B.C. and maintained their popularity for over a thousand years. Rediscovered in modern times, his story is just as stirring and profound as it was over 4000 years ago.

That rediscovery along with the amazing advances in archeology have opened a fascinating window into the ancient world of the land between the Tigris and Euphrates rivers, where what we know as civilization had its earliest beginnings, and done much to verify and give added context to that other great window on those times, the Pentateuch, which makes up the first five books of the Christian Bible.

I became aware of the changing face of ancient history about 15 years ago, when a friend of mine gave me a subscription to *Biblical Archeological Review* as a birthday gift. This marvelous magazine was full of glossy color photos of artifacts and digs throughout the near-east. I was enthralled, and soon was raiding used book stores and abusing the interlibrary loan program for anything on the subject I could lay hands on.

In the meantime I was also writing fiction. I had had written a few stories for a gaming company and had an historical spy novel making the rounds of agents. It takes a very long time for agents and publishers to tell you no, and I started filling that time with smaller writing projects. One day I was sitting in my office and an image came to me, of a warrior after a battle, sitting among the dead, weeping. I wrote down the scene, then spent several days puzzling out how that warrior got there and who she was. I had so much fun during the process that I decided to write the story in the same way, as a circular puzzle piece. The result was originally titled "A Matter of Will" but after passing through the re-write filter a few times became "Voice of the Spoiler" from a line from Lord Byron.

I would like to say the rest was history, and editors lined up to buy my masterwork, but sadly, that wasn't the case. Marion Zimmer Bradley wrote a fairly harsh rejection (but at least she read it!) and Algis Budrys, who got a further revised version, turned it down for his magazine with an "almost" but included a couple of paragraphs of suggestions for improvements. I made the suggested changes and... life got in the way, and my fiction writing career got put on hold for over a decade as I divorced, moved to another city, remarried, and reestablished my life.

One day Thomas, my oldest son, called me up and invited me to the Seattle Nebula Awards. We had a blast. He met many of his favorite writers, and I made friends with folks who were relentless in their insistence that I write fiction again, not because the world was crying out for my stories, but because encouraging other writers is one of the wonderful aspects of the writing community. By coincidence I was in Chicago for the Nebulas the next year, and the pressure became pretty hard to resist, especially from Lee Martindale, who slings a mean tale and as a member of the SFWA Musketeers slings an even meaner blade.

Within a few months I had half a dozen stories in circulation to various magazines, including another re-write of "Voice" which was accepted for publication by Bill Snodgrass for *The Sword Review*, an online magazine of fantasy and science fiction. It ran in October of 2005, along with another story of mine written specifically for the magazine's first Halloween issue.

"Voice of the Spoiler" was well received and got a nice review from *Tangent Online*. I moved on to other stories, but a few months later it was nominated for a readers' poll and did very well. Several people asked for a sequel. I resisted, but not too hard. The result was "The Servant of the Manthycore" which also appeared in *The Sword Review*, got an even better review in *Tangent* and finished a couple of places higher in the same annual readers' poll.

I wrote three more.

When I turned the last one in, Bill Snodgrass wrote me and asked if I would like to run the whole series in consecutive issues, and then printed as a chapbook. I agreed, but in the time between I kept writing, and the project grew up to be an episodic novel, an almost accidental book.

Along the way I was forced to learn a whole bunch of things, about writing, about horses, about history, and about languages. One of the biggest joys in this project was the amount of research some of the simplest things required. Remember the scene where Miri asked for a comb, and Ota-Emar's people bathed her? It sent me frantically researching soap. Did they have it? Was it tallow-based or oil based? Was it a luxury or a common item? Did it work in cold water? Turns out that they did have soap. It was made with alkali, water and cassia oil. It was a trade item, and was sometimes kept in clay cylinders. Oil based, it was more like modern liquid hand soap, and wouldn't smell bad like tallow soap. Cassia oil seemed familiar, so more research. Cassia is related to cinnamon, with a similar taste but stronger. It was also used as a flavoring in beer, no doubt creating feeble alibis for Bronze Age husbands coming home late from the tavern. "Honey, I stopped off at the public bath, must have swallowed some soap!" I am told by the way, on good authority, that this excuse would never have flown.

So, Ota's people would have had soap, oil-based so no heating of water was needed, and when she was finished Miri smelled nice. Of course all that made it into the story was the smell nice part. But the research was fun, and provided me with a perfectly justified excuse to do what writers call "cat vacuuming," which is using your writing time doing anything *but* writing.

Learning about bronze weapons and fighting was another chance to exfoliate the feline. Bronze is very hard, but very brittle. Swords were much shorter than later weapons made of iron. This size limit and the fragility of the weapons made for a completely different style of combat. Sword-to-sword contact was likely to result in a broken weapon, and shields were made with large metal bosses in the center and a hard rim just for that reason. Attacks were made over the shield or under. Excavations of Bronze Age battle sites reveal skeletons with bronze fragments in shoulder, collar and hip bones, which meant even winning could result in a broken weapon.

Try holding a bronze sword, if you get the opportunity. Any good sword feels like it is almost alive, but while a steel sword feels quick and lively, a bronze sword feels more solid, almost sullen, a bull mastiff to the iron blade's greyhound. A friend of mine compared a bronze sword he once held to a "lethal cricket-bat". The one I own feels heavy, and very businesslike. Fighting with a weapon like that was nothing like modern fencing; it was quick, brutal and ugly.

Bronze Age Mesopotamia is about the richest historical background I can imagine. It is the birthplace of the religions of half the people in the world. Abraham, the patriarch of Judaism, Christianity and Islam, was from Ur. His offstage appearance in the story takes place around 1800 B.C. during a time when there were literally thousands of gods worshipped in that part of the world. The Hittites alone claimed a thousand. The world view was simultaneously sophisticated and very, very strange to a modern reader, yet so many stories correspond to familiar accounts of the Torah and Old Testament that the strangeness is somehow rendered comprehensible. Gilgamesh wrestles a lion, as does Sampson. There is a great flood, with an ark and a gathering of the beasts and birds.

This congruence has permitted me to do what Bill Snodgrass calls "God Pointing" which is to introduce as a core to the story some of my Christian beliefs and morals. Ninshi travels with biblical characters, and her journey is punctuated with opportunities for redemption. Her story is about the choices she makes, and her rejection of what she knows to be true. That she rejects while still believing makes her tale a tragic one. For her the definition in Hebrews of faith as "the evidence of things not seen" is sadly reversed. She has seen and believes, but will not give up the very thing she hates the most, for fear of losing that which, in the end, she surrenders anyway.

Names and language have been fun, too. There are three major languages to play with, related but not always structured the same. Most of my linguistic research has been online. It sometimes amazes me that I am using the internet to access some of the earliest known writing, set down by the high-tech gurus of 4000 years ago using state of the art mud tablets and simple markings not much different in use and intent than the binary code at the heart of the computer I am writing this on.

I have to confess I have sometimes been lazy. There are many king-lists available, with hundreds of wonderfully strange names like Ashurbanipal and Shallim-ahhe. The latter, you will be happy to know, was one of the "Kings whose eponyms are destroyed" according to Assyrian King List. Better that than Ushpia, who sadly was one of the "Kings who lived in tents." Although I did not steal those specific names, many of the names in the story were taken from similar lists, sometimes modified slightly. To the true Sumerian, Assyrian and Hittite geeks out there, I apologize, because, as you know I did take occasional liberties. If it interferes with your enjoyment of the story, just think of the offending word or name as a local usage.

Many people have helped me along the way. I would like to start my thanks with my son Thomas, who set me back on the path of fiction writing. All of my children contributed in one way or another, but there are many of them, so in the interests of space I'll thank them as a group. John Kono was the first reader of the tale, 15 years ago, and has contributed historical help along the way. I am a member of STEW, a writers' group based in Seattle, and its members Nisi Shawl, John Aegard, Victoria Garcia, Mike Canfield, Sabrina Chase and Mike Toot have helped make this story stronger and tighter, as did the members of my online group the Dragons Den, R. S. Leergaard, J.J. Fellows, Daniel Ausema, Barbara A. Barnett, Celina Summers and the rest.

Berry Sizemore gets special thanks for arranging the introduction by Michael Moorcock, and for making killer chicken sandwiches. Mike turned out to be a great guy to talk to, as well, and the intro he wrote had me walking on air for days. Elizabeth Ann Scarborough taught me tons about writing, and has been a great friend through the process. Lois Tilton endured an early draft, and still was kind enough to write a blurb, and if there is a sweeter person in the writing world than Vera Nazarian, who also wrote a blurb, then I haven't met them. I have already mentioned Nisi Shawl, but she deserves extra mention because of all of my friends who have helped me grow as a writer, she has been the chief cultivator, and she also made time to write kind things. Bill Snodgrass has kept me on task and this was his idea to start with, and without the amazing illustrations by Rachel Marks this book would be a poorer thing.

Always, always I am grateful for the support and love of my beautiful wife, without whom this journey would be far less sweet.

Michael Ehart

Michael Ehart has been at various times all of the expected things: laborer, seminary student, musician, shoe salesman, political consultant, teacher, diaper truck driver, stand-up comedian, and the least important guy with an office at a movie studio. He currently works as a computer systems engineer. His first magazine sale was at the age of 15, which means he has been writing for nearly 40 years, with occasional breaks for gainful employment.

He lives in the upper left hand corner of the United States with his wife Shaharazahd and his youngest son, Alexander.

Rachel Marks is a homeschooling mom to four beautiful kids. She divides her time between her drawing table and the computer desk, working as both an illustrator and writer in her spare moments. She also had the privilege of being managing editor for the Christian Literary Magazine, *Haruah*, and is currently working to publish her first novel.

You can read more about her on her webpage, < www.shadowofthewood.com >.

Printed in the United States
135114LV00001B/17/A

9 780979 307959